THE ANGELICS

WILDEST DREAMS

THE ANGELICS SERIES
BOOK ONE

DR. HEATHER KRISTIAN STRANG

For more information, or to access the resources in this book, visit:

http://www.Sacred-Spirituality.org

Receive a free *The Angelics: Wildest Dreams* Playlist to listen to before, during and after reading.

As a thank you for saying "yes" to this book, we're gifting you with a free Angelics Playlist to dance to, groove to, and enjoy!

You can also choose to be the first to know when *The Angelics: Afterlife* (Book 2 in the series) and other books from Dr. Heather Kristian Strang are available.

Get it all here: **bit.ly/angelicsplaylist**

"*Important encounters are planned by the souls long before the bodies see each other.*"

"*You don't have to explain your dreams, they belong to you.*"

"*It's the possibility of having a dream come true that makes life interesting.*" -Paulo Coelho

PROLOGUE

Theirs was a life of orgasmic ecstasy. Every day, united together, they enjoyed the unadulterated, pure bliss of living and being as One. It was a good life. It could even be said it was the best life. It was a life of magical, heavenly unfoldings while assisting the Angelic realm.

"Can you imagine a better way to be than this?" they breathed into each other. They could not.

And so for eons they lived in this Way, as two Souls of golden light that lived as One. Then, most unexpectedly, they were summoned to a special meeting with Source HerSelf. This was unusual, as meetings with Source were reserved for new assignments to other realms and promotions to expanded service areas. They hadn't met with Source in many ages and had not received any extended guidance that they would be moving on to a new realm. It was unnecessary they felt as they relished their work in the Angelic realm; it was richly rewarding and nourishing.

They entered the space that Source indicated She would be at for their meeting. It was one of their favorite places in the Angelic realm, the garden of the Highest Light. They knew Source had entered the garden as they felt the most sublime peace and heavenly grace encircle them. As She began speaking, they could hear Her voice beaming all around them, caressing them with Her lyrical expression. Sparkles of golden light filled the garden and the air smelled of rosebuds.

"We have enjoyed witnessing your glorious union as One in these realms," Source HerSelf spoke. "You have been of great service here in your creation of other worlds within the Angelic realm as well as in your assistance to other Angels who are traveling on assignment. But now, your love, light and bliss are needed in another, more material part of the Universe."

Excitement and trepidation rippled through them at hearing these words from Source HerSelf. They had not focused solely on one material plane outside of the Angelic realm in centuries. What might be required of them? They could separate their energies whenever they needed to, but they preferred to stay united as one large golden orb of Light, which contained within it all that they were and ever would be.

"It's the Earth plane that's in desperate need of your help and we'll be sending you there most immediately," Source communicated.

They gasped. *Oh no, not Earth.* They had heard reports of the despair encompassing the plane of consciousness known as Earth and how the beings there were fully disconnected from both their own Sacred Wisdom and The Divine. This disconnection had nearly ruined the entire Spirit and matter that Earth was and is.

"We are so grateful to receive a new assignment, as always, Oh Holy One. However, Earth? We are not certain our gifts of creation, Light and Divine Love could penetrate the intense despair of that plane. Perhaps there's another realm that we could be of higher benefit to?"

Source HerSelf paused, as if considering the question, and for a moment, they felt hopeful for an assignment more to their delight.

"It is true the stories you've heard about the Earth, Beloved

One. It was taken over by beings from a disconnected-from-Source realm long ago. And because some of the humans gave consent in exchange for promises of magnificent power, wealth, and agelessness–myself, the Earth Creators, the ones known as Mother-Father God, and the Angelic realm could not interfere."

Exactly right, they thought. Therefore, there would be no reason to send them to the Earth realm when the humans had willfully chosen to live a life of suffering, disconnected from The Divine.

"However," Source continued, "what you may not know is that at the time of this takeover, an agreement was made with these beings. While we could not interfere, we *could* create a new agreement with these ones, in the hopes of someday assisting the Earth in Her full illumination. It is, of course, our superlative desire for all planes of consciousness, including Earth, to thrive and for Her inhabitants to live a blissful life of creative harmony.

"And so, we formed an agreement with the beings that included timeline checkpoints. We would then reconvene to see if a tipping point was reached of humans who chose The Divine over the artificial. This, you might call the artificial matrix, which is devoid of Earth-based and Divine-based creations. Of course, the beings were certain humans would never choose The Divine when distracted by the many desires of the flesh thrown at them, not to mention the distraction of being integrated into artificial intelligence. And this is why the negative agenda energies agreed to such checkpoints in the first place–they never believed humans would choose their own Divine liberation.

"Even so, the final checkpoint in this agreement is fast approaching–the year known on Earth as 2020. Per this agreement, if by this time, 22 percent or more of the Earth's human population are vibrating in harmony with The Divine, the negative forces will lose their power, and their creations of slavery and suffering will slowly collapse until they no longer remain on Earth. From there, the beings will have no choice but to return to their home plane of consciousness or be reintegrated into the void."

They shuddered, their shared energy field growing smaller at the thought of such a disconnected place. Why ever would anyone go there, they wondered quietly to themselves. But they had little time to ponder this as Source continued speaking.

"And so, the Earth Creators known as Mother-Father God and myself have decided that you will enter the Earth realm. You will be split into two energies and the feminine aspect of you will be born in the year known as 1978. The masculine aspect of you will come onto Earth in the year known as 1980. You'll have up to forty years to reunite with one another and create a bandwidth of Love, Light, and well-being so vast that it assists the humans in choosing The Divine over the hijacked, distorted agenda. Who humans truly are is a Divine creation, but due to the takeover of the Earth, along with the poisoning of the human body and Soul, most do not consciously know this.

"As you've heard, and as the reports show, this agenda has resulted in a race of beings who are in the majority devoid of The Divine and because of this, they suffer tremendously. They remain imprisoned on Earth because of this hijacking and cannot fully leave the Earth realm if they do not awaken to the truth of who they are and of what All-That-Is, is. It's imperative that you go to Earth to assist these ones oh, Beloved One. All those who choose The Divine in their lifetime will be set free of the slave system and will return to Earth as free beings or travel to other planes of consciousness for creation and growth."

All that the great Holy One Source HerSelf was sharing became a blur because they could not move past the portion where She mentioned they would split into halves and then have up to forty Earth years to reunite. Split into halves? Reunite?! They were never not able to be One. How could this be?!

4

"Oh, Great Source? We do have a question for you. What is this about splitting into feminine and masculine halves and reuniting that you mentioned? Won't we go to Earth as One, as we are now, as we primarily choose to be, to assist the humans in their remembering of The Divine and to assist in their subsequent freedom from slavery? We know that we can separate our energies but we prefer not ever to do this unless absolutely necessary."

"This is a wise question and I'm happy you asked it," Source responded. "On Earth, you will incarnate as two separate beings, as this is the way of the humans. You will enter human bodies or avatars that are created in the image and likeness of the Creators of Earth, the ones known as God/Goddess or Mother-Father God. And so, one of you will carry the action-oriented, create-in-form God frequency as your primary frequency and the other will incarnate carrying the visionary, spiritual Goddess frequency as your primary frequency. Mother-Father God were quite brilliant and ensured that both these frequencies inhabited each form, with one serving as a primary energy and the other as a sub-prime energy, just as it is for them. Then, on Earth, two beings carrying these primary energies come together as a complement to one another. They unify their lives and bodies and live as one, in two separate forms. This is as close to unity as the humans can experience while in their Earth bodies. While it's not at the same level of union as you experience here, it is quite blissful, even for a realm like Earth."

While they innerstood what Source was sharing with them, they were aghast by the prospect of being separated in such a dramatic and what seemed to them cruel fashion on Earth. The fact that humans were separated into masculine and feminine forms, was most shocking as all beings were all things. Didn't humans know this? To limit oneself into one form, separate from their Divine Counterpart was not only unusual, but they were concerned it could be impossible for them to navigate, especially without one another the whole way through. How much despair would they experience living separately from one another for upwards of forty Earth years? What kind of mistakes would they naturally make without the other half of their being-ness with them? As all of this coursed through them, Source carried on.

"There's something though that's quite concerning to us, besides the obvious with the takeover of the Earth realm. Many Earth beings unite with the incorrect energy–meaning they create unions with beings that are not the Love of their Life or, as is the case for you as Angelics, the other half of their Soul. This creates extreme discord on Earth. There's much betrayal because without a connection to The Divine, these ones have not unified with their true Beloved or other half of themselves in form." Source seemed to sigh after sharing this.

"This is utterly horrifying. They must be so confused without each other and they must make such terrible decisions. We cannot fathom this."

"It's true," Source said. "This is exactly what occurs. It's hard to witness, and yet, each human Soul can choose The Divine or choose the artificial matrix that's present on Earth. That's why we need you there to be a guiding Light as we near the benchmark we put into place long ago. Less than 22 percent of humans are using their free will to choose The Divine and thus break the spell of the hijacked agenda. Mother-Father God has asked for us to send in a unique and important group of Angelics to assist with improving their final numbers. As you can imagine, a unified Angelic couple has more impact than any human, which is why you're needed. Your specific mission, Beloved One, will be to unite with one another after being split into two human forms and then assist other humans to raise their frequency so they may find their Beloved love as well.

"It's quite complex on Earth, so many Souls will not be ready for this or will have other levels of relating to do before coming into their deepest and highest Sacred Union. In any event, your work is to help as many of them as you can in the most creative of ways so that they may transcend the agenda and suffering-based Earth matrix and be restored to freedom and bliss, which is the state the Earth most wishes to experience."

"If you believe in our ability to do this, we will of course do so Oh Holy One. Thank you for choosing us for this mission. We will need all of our Angelic family members on standby to assist us from the realm while we navigate the many hurdles that Earth presents. We intend to unite as quickly as we can upon incarnating and we trust that we will be supported in doing so."

It was then that they felt a gigantic swooshing of air circle around them like a warm hug, while unique spiraled sparkles rained down upon them and throughout the garden of Light. Their unified field glowed ever more brightly from their encounter with Source.

And while they were honored to be amongst a select number of Angelics sent for this mission on Earth, they were quite concerned about what being split into human halves would entail and how it would affect them.

CHAPTER 1

Veronica Walter's bright green eyes popped open. She surveyed her heavenly white fluffy pillows and white cozy blankets and blinked a few times. She was surrounded by filled-to-the-brim white bookcases against every wall, her books carefully organized by genre and theme. Anyone stepping into her room might have imagined they were in a book heaven of sorts.

It had been a weird–but nice–dream. She blinked a few more times to try to remember what had happened. She had been floating far away, up in the sky, encased in a beautiful, peaceful, love-filled golden light. Everything felt light and easy and ... free. Another energy was there with her, too, who felt sweet, blissful, and innately like another version of herself, only masculine. He stirred the most delicious sensations in her. They were wrapped up together in an embrace that wasn't like any embrace she'd ever had before. It was more like a merging of their Souls. It seemed so familiar that it almost made her want to go back to sleep so she could reunite with him in that expanded and dreamy state again.

That was hardly an option though since she had to hustle to her job at the local bookstore, Books on the Beach. But first, she needed coffee. Veronica jumped out of bed, scooting herself to the kitchen in her tie-dye green pajama pants and white tank top, black curls piled on top of her head.

"Well, good morning sleepy head," her sister Margot teased.

Her big sister Margot was always up early. Her job as the leading real estate agent on the Oregon Coast practically required it. Margot had not only been up for a while, but she had also already had her coffee and a phone meeting with a client. She was as bubbly as ever and thoroughly enjoyed teasing Veronica whenever she could.

While Veronica wouldn't describe her and Margot as complete opposites, they nearly looked unrelated. It often shocked people that they were sisters, only two years apart. Margot kept her dark locks in disguise, dyeing her hair for years a golden blonde. She also had her curls blown out, and you'd never catch her without an organic airbrushed tan and fake, yet tasteful eyelashes, both of which made her green eyes (the one thing she and Veronica *did* have in common) stand out in a way that took most men's breath away. Margot's style was form-fitting business suits with sexy heels or skin-baring athleisure. Her nails were manicured and painted to perfection, mostly in colors named after some of her favorite alcoholic drinks, like pina colada and strawberry daiquiri. Margot had been the homecoming queen and the small-town beauty that everyone loved. She'd never left the Oregon Coast and didn't see any reason she ever would. Life there was very, very good to her.

"I'm surprised you're still here and not out closing multi-million-dollar deals at–what time is it?" Veronica leaned over the black and white granite kitchen island to glimpse the oven clock. "At 9 a.m., isn't that when all the multi-million-dollar deals happen, sis?"

Margot was well-known throughout Oregon due to her successful billboards featured along the Oregon Coastline and anywhere tourism on the Oregon Coast was promoted. She had done Veronica a big sister favor by letting her rent a room in her four-bedroom, three-bathroom oceanfront beach palace on the cliffs overlooking the Pacific Ocean outside of Depoe Bay while Veronica got back on her feet. This was generous for many reasons, including that Margot typically lived alone so she wouldn't be interrupted from the many men who were blessed enough to be invited into her bed. She had made an exception for her sister.

"Haha, Ronni, very cute. You should know that the multi-million-dollar deals happen over cocktails or a bowl of our famous coastal clam chowder. If you must know, I had to work from home this morning because I had to see Ryan off." She smiled brightly at the mention of his name.

"What?! He stayed the whole night?" Thankfully, despite Margot's abundance of men, her home had the perfect layout for their roomie situation. Their bedrooms were located on opposite ends, and both their bedrooms were en suite, which meant they weren't *always* in one another's space. This also meant Veronica didn't have real-time access to all the comings and goings of the men that Margot loved, but she did know that they rarely spent the entire night. Thankfully what Veronica *did* have real-time access to was the stunning coastal views that laid out before them, from almost every window.

"I'm thinking he might be the one," Margot mused as she sipped her second cup of morning coffee. "For right now, anyway." She winked at her sister. "I mean, he's not as rich as me, but close. He's *very* successful in commercial real estate in Portland and is starting to expand along the Coast. We have so much fun together and the sex is AAAAAHHHHMMMAAAZZZZZINNNGGGG."

"Well, you need to give me every last detail, because you know that ever since Ben and I broke up, I can barely even look at another man without crying. For now, living vicariously through your abundant sex life will have to do."

Veronica had thought she and Ben would go the distance. He was a good man and they both seemed to want the same things. He supported her bookstore owner dream, while she worked at a variety of her favorite bookstores to learn the ins-and-outs, and she supported his water-skiing passion. They loved to grill with friends on the weekends and until six months ago, they had lived together quite happily–she had thought anyway–in the big city lights of Portland. But that had all come crashing down when Veronica found a series of intimate emails between him and his best friend, Susie. Turned out there was more than friendship happening there. While Ben tried to explain that it wasn't Veronica's fault (not that she had assumed it was, she had wanted to add), he had a stronger, more intense connection with Susie that he simply couldn't deny any longer.

And so, here she was living with her big sister at thirty-six, wondering when her bookstore-owning dream would materialize and when she would ever meet the other half of her Soul, if that kind of love even existed for her. She had abandoned that dream of Soul love in her late teens after Bryan, her sixteen-year-old love had dumped her for a girl who *would* have sex with him. Veronica just wasn't ready then and had asked him for patience and time. He opted for finding a girl who would give him what he wanted. Crushed, Veronica decided then and there that Soul love wouldn't happen for her. Although if she was honest, over the years she had always hoped that somehow she was wrong. That somehow her Soulmate would be revealed to her.

"Ronni, did you hear me?? I said he fell asleep immediately after..."

Veronica's eyes came into focus as she noticed Margot rising from the black leather high-back chair at the kitchen island. With a snap of her fingers, Margot grabbed her sister's attention. Veronica had been idly standing beside the Miele espresso machine, intending to make herself a cup of coffee. However, she had been too preoccupied with her thoughts to proceed.

"Oh sorry Margot, I was zoning out as I noticed the

glaringly obvious lack of sex, love, and money in my current sitch. Thanks for that reminder btws. On another note, have you ever wanted to be in a relationship with the other half of your Soul? Or have you ever wanted that instead of hot Ryan and his hot body and all your hot sex?"

"Well, of course." Her sister sighed, exasperated. "*Every* woman wants that Ronni, but only a small select few get to have that kind of love. You gotta pull your head out of the clouds, honey. Ever since you were little, you talked about Soulmates. And while it's a cute thought, it's not a realistic one—just look at what happened with Bryan when you were sixteen and then Ben in your thirties. And let's not even talk about the other varied jerk-faces you dated in your twenties."

Veronica rolled her eyes, although she couldn't disagree entirely with her sister. Margot saw she was getting through to her and decided to take things a step further. She strode over to Veronica, holding her second and third cups of coffee in a large white and gold "Bad Boss Bitch" mug as if proximity would drive her point home. Veronica slowly and playfully backed away, moving over to the fridge to grab some creamer for her own vat of coffee. Margot giggled and moved back to her chair at the island to continue her lecture.

"You see, Ronni, a wealthy, stable man who loves you is plenty. Not everyone gets to live the ideal fantasy. It's like I've been telling you—especially since the Ben debacle—let go of the fantasy and join me as a realtor. Let's make you some money, honey. Let's make this the last time you rent a room showing up with nothing but boxes of books and a few suitcases. Listen, I can be your broker and you can start making real money, and then one of the many eligible real estate brokers located anywhere here in Oregon can be your love. Besides, you're gonna be forty in four years. You can't keep wishing on a star or hoping some magical angel is going to show up and grant you your dream life. Owning a bookstore and making any money doing it while being in a relationship with the other half of your

Soul is just not gonna happen. I'm sorry to break it to you, sis. You gotta get real and start creating a life that will pay you well, let you take some nice vacations every year, and give you plenty of good sex and laughter."

Of course, Veronica had heard this diatribe by Margot all before. For years her sister had encouraged her to pull her nose out of books and relationships that weren't "serving" her and get into the land of making money and a good-enough relationship. She had listened to her sister on the relationship front by even being with Ben she had thought. While he was a good guy, it wasn't as though he was the love of her life—she was self-aware enough to know that. She had been willing to settle for good sex, stability and laughter, but even that had burned her. So, was she back to pining for a Soulmate since settling had ended in disaster for her as well? Before she could even answer that question for herself, she had to also own that she was having a difficult time giving up her dream of being a bookstore owner. She imagined filling her shop with not only books, but also gemstones and other magical items.

Ever since she was a little girl, gemstones and, oddly, white feathers had fascinated her. She also wanted to offer poetry, storytelling, and open mic nights at her shop and create a community where creativity and the love of story flourished. Veronica could see this bookstore vision so vividly in her mind; it had been with her ever since she could remember. Anytime she would daydream as a child, she would picture a bookstore. In it, hovered a faint vision of a man, unlike any man she had ever known, who glowed and whose irises were surrounded by gold light. She had thought of him throughout her life and had seen his outline in her imagination. But it was a daydream and everyone knows those don't come true she chided herself. As a little girl, she had felt she had a Soulmate, but now it seemed the best she could hope for was a raise at the bookstore she worked at and a man who didn't end up dumping her for his best friend.

"I know you only want to see me happy, Margot, but for the five-millionth time, there's no way I could be a realtor. I don't have the technical skills needed or the interest to learn the business. So, with that being said, please excuse me as I go get ready for my non-glamourous, but fun and rewarding job at Books on the Beach," she added in a fake English accent, hoping to lighten the mood and get Margot off her "join me as a realtor and settle for a decent man" soapbox.

"Okay, okay, fine. Have a great day Ronni doing your little book thang, and you let me know if you change your mind," Margot raised a strawberry daiquiri red painted fingernail and pointed at Veronica in the way only a big sister can. "Oh, by the way, this was in the mail for you." She tossed over an oversized direct mail piece that had Veronica's name on it and sauntered out the door.

Veronica picked it up, curious. Most of the direct marketing pieces came in Margot's name because she owned the house, and Veronica wasn't much for signing up for random shopping lists. It was a mailer from The Starlight Theater up the coast, advertising a local indie band that had made it big, returning for a hometown concert. Hmm...it seemed interesting. Maybe she could tear Margot away from real estate and the bedroom with Ryan for a weekend up the coast. Strange that it would come addressed to her, though. She took the postcard with her and tossed it on her nightstand while she got dressed.

CHAPTER 2

When she reached the bookstore, the owner, Henry, was already there going through a new book order. Stacks of books piled all around the tall oak desk, while Henry's tabby cat Melvin carefully paraded through each stack, his long tail curling upwards as he made his way through the books. Henry had meticulously sorted them according to his own methodical system, in preparation for their upload into the online inventory system.

In his early fifties, Henry was boyishly handsome with salt and pepper flecked black hair with a slight receding hairline. He kept his hair short, highlighting his strong jaw and the jubilant smile that could often be found on his face. He had a lean, tall build and a jovial nature that made him magnetic to others. He started Books on the Beach fifteen years ago and had created a cult following of happy customers.

Books on the Beach was a former cozy cabin converted into a bookstore, located a few blocks from the roaring waves of the Pacific Ocean in Newport, Oregon. Comfortable, well-worn caramel leather armchairs and love seats were tucked throughout the four rooms and upstairs loft filled floor-to-ceiling with books. A rustic fireplace stayed well stoked throughout the colder winter, spring and fall months in the great room area and added a nice ambiance in the summer months when Henry filled it with large cylinder cream candles instead of firewood.

Books on the Beach, a staple in the community, was the place to find new releases and an eclectic mix of books covering a spectrum of metaphysical topics, including everything from extraterrestrials to chanting and mantras to the healing power of herbs and high-vibrational foods.

"Hey, there, Veronica, I'm gonna get these new books in the system and then I'll have you put them out. But first, can you get these postcards up on the community board and on the front tables by the entrance?"

Henry handed her a stack of postcards–the exact same card that her sister had given her earlier that morning. This time, she took a closer look. The Sunshine State was the name of the band, and Veronica found it quite ironic if they were truly from Oregon. It obviously was a wise decision to wait until the end of spring at the Coast before holding their concert. It would definitely increase their chances of having better weather and catching more actual sunshine.

"Playing for the first time in ten years in their hometown," the oversized postcard read. "Let's give a hearty Oregon welcome to the most famous musical ensemble to come from the Oregon Coast. Join us June 11 at 7 p.m."

Small text bubbles surrounded a photo of the band, three men who gazed smolderingly back at the camera. The postcard said they had been featured on The Tonight Show, headlined a major worldwide stadium tour, and had topped the Billboard Top 10 for seven years in a row. Impressive, especially coming from the rural Oregon Coast. Veronica didn't recall ever hearing about them, but she chalked that up to having lived in Portland for most of her life, and only recently coming to the Coast. As Veronica hung up the information on the community board, she had a slight, almost urgent thought pop into her head that she should buy tickets before they sold out. She thought it odd as it was only May, which made the show a month away, and it was hardly high tourist season at the coast...

～

"They sold out! Did you hear Ronni?" Margot screamed as she entered the house that night after work. "People are flying in from all over the world to go to this hometown show. I only know because I had a couple of my millionaire clients' assistants calling me like rabid super fans to ask about nice homes to rent for that weekend."

How strange that everyone seemed to be so excited about this concert with a trio Veronica had never heard of. The Oregon Coast in general was super sleepy and most people visited from the city to get away–to stroll the beach, play board games with their family, hike coastal trails, and rest. The coast was almost a vortex for relaxation. It was the perfect place to spend a weekend doing nothing other than reading a book, walking in the rain, whale-watching or spending an afternoon picking up unique rocks and shells. There wasn't much nightlife, as most of the coast closed down by 9 p.m., save for a slew of dive bars that fishermen, loggers, and locals frequented.

Veronica was curled up in her old Lululemon black leggings and a blue ribbed tank on the cozy slate grey lounger in the living room, rereading one of her old fan favorites, *And Then There Were None* by the legendary–Agatha Christie. She propped her hand under her chin and looked over at her sister who had plopped down on the matching loveseat facing her. As always Margot was impeccably dressed, this time in a black miniskirt with black tights, heels and a black and velvet purple lined jacket. She looked like the badass realtor she was, Veronica thought to herself.

"Ah well, guess we won't be able to go then. I was kind of hoping I could get you and Ryan to go with me if I could pry you two from the bedroom, that is. You know, as your little sister I need to suss out if he really has the potential to be 'the one for now' for you, and the only way to do that would be to observe you in a neutral habitat where you weren't having sex all the time," Veronica smirked.

"Well, sister, turns out your wildest dreams are about to come true, because BONUS, one of my real estate broker friends, gave me four tickets, with VIP mezzanine seats to go to the show. And so that you're not a lonely third wheel, I invited Bryce from my office to go with us."

Veronica groaned. Bryce, again? He was nice and maybe even handsome, but Veronica wasn't ready to waste time on another man who would eventually fall for someone else, or who she would have to get to know, meet his family and do all the relationship things required of her, only to be let down. And since Margot was positive there was no Soulmate available for someone as common as Veronica (and she didn't fully disagree with her), then she was going to find a way to get comfy with her beloved books and maybe add some cats to the mix, and then call it a life.

Not that Margot would even consider allowing her to *have* a cat at her stunningly beautiful and white (everything in Margot's home was pure white) oceanside palace. Instead, Veronica had to get her fix from Henry's bookstore cat Melvin. He notoriously loved hopping up on the checkout counter when she was helping customers, and she found that the sight of him made her happy.

"Margot! You know I'm not interested in Bryce. I told you that the last time you invited him out with us–on the down-low, no less–to join us for the bonfire at the beach last month. God, you're aggravating!"

"I know, I know, you say that, but Bryce is a patient guy, and he thinks you're incredibly fascinating and preettttyyyy." Margot drew out *pretty* as if a boy thinking a girl was pretty was so captivating and exciting that Veronica would suddenly decide she wanted to date him. Besides, wasn't there something more to relationships than job-interviewing one another to see if they'd be compatible for a lifetime of family events, life struggles, and sex?

Veronica shook her head at her sister as she got up from the lounger in a huff, walking into the kitchen to the hot water kettle to make her nightly organic chamomile tea from a farm not too far from their home. She sighed in annoyance, tapping her fingers on the counter as the water boiled. When would her sister stop pushing her agenda onto her?!

Margot must have realized she would have to double down on her big sister tough-love-ness to get Veronica to cave on this imposed double date. She got up from the couch and made her way over to Veronica in the kitchen. She stood face to face with her sister as the tea kettle rolled to a boil.

"Listen, Ronni, you've got one month to get excited about this. The concert sold out in less than a day and it's going to be an amazing show. You rarely go out if you aren't working at that bookstore or holed up here reading, and frankly, it's difficult to watch. You've been broken up with Ben, which I know was traumatic for you, for almost six months. It's time to go out and have some fun. Is it so wrong that I want to see my sister happy and fulfilled? Or at least well-sexed?" Margot giggled, putting her arm around her sister.

Veronica burst out laughing. If she didn't immediately go for whatever crazy fiasco her sister was trying to coax her into, Margot would always default to Rambo big sister mode. It was both adorable and frustrating. Margot had been the leader of their pack for so long, she knew all the buttons to push. Veronica also couldn't ignore the small voice within her that encouraged her to appease her sister as she usually did—even though she might show up for this date kicking and screaming.

"Okay, okay, it will be fun to go out with you guys, and you know I love going to see live music, even if it's a band I've never heard of. I just don't know why you had to invite Bryce." She poured the boiling water into her favorite white and brown local pottery mug, watching as the tea ball bobbed up and down. She looked up at her sister curious to see how she would justify the obvious interference of inviting Bryce.

"You know I invited him to keep things interesting, girl. I cannot let you waste away over here with your fortieth birthday looming before you!"

Veronica guffawed. "Please! My fortieth birthday is hardly looming, Margot."

Veronica took her tea back with her to her cozy lounge spot, hoping to end the conversation altogether. She curled up on the lounger, setting her tea carefully on the starfish coaster on the espresso end table. "I have a solid four-well, three-and-a-half years to go. You should be worried about your own self, you turn forty before I do, if you remember correctly sis. And besides, who cares if I'm forty and I haven't met the love of my life and I still work at a bookstore? Like, who does that even hurt?"

Margot clucked her tongue in annoyance as she opened the fridge, grabbing a gingerberry kombucha and returning to face her sister in the living room. She stood over her, the kombucha in one hand, the other placed on her hip. "First of all sis, I'm making my bread and I'm enjoying a steady stream of men, in perhaps a never-ending partner application process. I like it that way. I can soar into my forties with all of my business handled. It's you I'm worried about. And like I've said to you a million times, let go of any notion of epic, once-in-a-lifetime love, Ronni. Let's remember this. You want stable, supportive, financially successful, good sex, and laughter–the core tenets of any worthwhile relationship. And being a successful real estate agent is quite easy with the right training. That's all you need. It's easy. You can do both and waltz into your forties with your head held high."

Margot had practically raised Veronica as their parents were otherwise unavailable, their dad chasing the next hot car and

21

girl, and their mother partying when she wasn't at one of her many minimum-wage paying gigs. Margot was always watching out for Veronica, all with cautious optimism. Veronica suspected that the little girl in Margot would not rest until Veronica was married off and making a good income, two things that Margot seemed convinced would mean her sister was stable, secure and cared for. Ironically, this was not exactly what Veronica wanted–well, at least not in the traditional ways. But she didn't dare try explaining that to Margot.

Margot interrupted Veronica's reverie again, with another brilliant big sister idea to help her floundering little sis. "You know what? I just remembered; I have this great book written by a gal who lives on the Coast. You should talk to Henry about carrying her books. A friend of mine gave it to me back when I was building my business several years ago. Even though, you know I'm not super into woo-woo stuff, the principles helped me manifest my first six-figure year and just kept skyrocketing from there. Anything that will help me make more money, I'm down for–even if it's the woo. Anyway, the book talks about the Law of Attraction and other metaphysical stuff that might help you out right now. I used it in my business, but I'm sure it could help you get into a more relaxed place around our double date at The Sunshine State concert, and who knows what else?"

Veronica narrowed her eyes and scowled back at her sister. She knew Margot's intentions were good, however irritating they might be.

"Ok, sure, yeah, I'll take a look. Maybe I'll use it to magnetize my own booooookstooooore," Veronica said to emphasize her commitment to her dream.

Margot smiled smugly as she turned in the other direction to go get the book for Veronica. "Sure, chica, use it for whatever you want."

Veronica got up, feeling like her yummy book reading time with Agatha Christie had been ruined by Margot's dating interference and lecture. She headed to her room, shouting down the hall as she did, "Hey, Margot, what kind of music does The Sunshine State play, anyway?"

"Oh, you know, indie, alt-rock or something like that. I think it's kind of like Everclear meets The Decemberists," she shouted back from down the hallway.

Veronica was curious and grabbed her phone from her messy, unmade bed to find the band on Spotify. What she wanted more than anything after that conversation was some good music along with a long, hot bath. Then, maybe she'd try to dive into one of her favorite books again. She connected her phone to a speaker, and the music from The Sunshine State filled her room while she went to run her bath.

A few minutes later, Margot knocked on her door, while simultaneously opening it (cuz siblings don't value privacy).

"Ronni?" she called.

Veronica popped out of the bathroom, make-up remover in hand, to see what she needed, and immediately Margot threw a book at her, catching her off guard.

"Ah, thanks sis, geesh!" she said, taking a closer look. The cover showed a photo of Haystack Rock in Pacific City with a young woman walking on the beach. Above it, read the title, *A Life of Magic: An Oracle for Spirit-Led Living*.

Veronica set the book on top of her "to read" book pile on the table next to her bed, careful not to knock over the photo of her and her best friend from college Eloise. Margot lingered, watching her.

"I see you're listening to The Sunshine State. Preparing for the concert, I like to see it sis. It's pretty good music, right?"

Veronica couldn't lie it wasn't hard to listen to, "Yeah, not bad–I love that they bring in the violin and cello too. Looks like it might be a good concert to go to after all."

Veronica stuck out her tongue and grabbed a white throw pillow to toss at Margot, who squealed and slammed the door shut.

Hand-in-hand, they ran down a long path in the forest. On each side of the path, there were doors, doors of all kinds. Some were intricately carved with wood designs, while others were basic office room doors, and still others were arched and made of stucco. Veronica caught a glimpse of a hobbit house door, as well as a mirrored door and one that looked like a portal to the void. She could feel that they could choose to open any door they wanted. It was simply a matter of which one they would choose.

Veronica felt so alive, almost invincible, with the power of his hand entwined with hers. What door would they open? Where would they go? What would they do?

They chose the third door on their left, telepathically communicating that this was the door that was most attractive to them. It was a rich cherry wood with black steel rods over it, keeping it closed. They both grabbed the rods at either end, lifting them to open the door. Once opened, they bounded forward, only to come to a screeching halt.

A heaviness filled the air, as tanks drove by and soldiers in full uniform walked and ran to various areas, guns in hand. Hitler's voice could be heard over a megaphone, and a dense mist clouded their eyes from seeing more. Instantly they knew this was not the place for them, and immediately whirled around, grabbing one another's hand, running back out through the open door. Once on the other side of the scene, they slammed the door behind them, putting the steel posts back in place and turned to run further down the forested door-laden path.

They kept running and the sun began to shine, as they moved to another door, this one royal blue with ornate carvings of blue jays in front of them...

Veronica jolted upright in her bed, her eyes popping open. She was buzzing with excitement, mixed with both fear and anticipation. This man was the same one from the dream she had a couple of weeks before where they were floating in some kind of etheric state–she was sure of it. He felt the same to her. She never had dreams like this, not that she could remember, anyway. She wanted to go back to sleep to spend more time with her mystery man in their surreal adventures.

Veronica laid back down, willing herself to fall back asleep. What was that war scene they had stepped into and that ever-long hallway of doors outside in the forest? Was it a metaphor? It seemed so real. Veronica couldn't shake the feeling that it *was* real, that she had raced down that hallway with him. After thirty minutes of insomnia, Veronica glanced over at her nightstand. The clock said 4:44 a.m. and she felt curious by the numerical sequence. She had noticed lately that whenever she looked at the clock now it was 2:22, 3:33 or 11:11. It struck her as odd, but she didn't know why.

She sighed. The concert was coming up in a couple of weeks, and that meant a date with Bryce. Was she ready? Did she even believe in love anymore? Would she be better off doing what her sister said by starting a more lucrative career and meeting a man that way?

Henry wasn't going to sell the bookstore anytime soon, and she didn't have the funds to start her own, even if he did. On top of that, she wouldn't want to compete with him. Veronica had made some progress forward by suggesting a monthly storytelling event that she would oversee. Henry seemed positive about her idea and encouraged her to put the event together to see how it resonated with their customers. At the very least, it seemed like a step in the right direction. To have her own store and home, she would have to make about ten-times what Henry was paying her, and he was paying her well. Or go back to waitressing part-time as she had done to supplement her income for years.

Her thoughts were interrupted by the ping of a text. She shouldn't have kept her phone on at night by her bed, but old habits were hard for her to break. It was from Bryce, "Super excited to see you at The Sunshine State show! Have you seen them play before?"

Wow, he was ever the eager one wasn't he, Veronica sassily thought. She quickly chided herself. Rather than being a smart-ass, she could instead lean into it. If her sister was right, she would have to learn how to get comfortable living something other than her fantasy life.

Besides, texting is how people get to know each other, and how they date, Veronica reminded herself. It wasn't as if she could sleep all day and night hanging out with the love that kept showing up in her dream state. She was going to have to do what everyone else did: start by texting, have a date, then have more dates, get to know each other until love grew. *If* it grew. Maybe she hadn't given Bryce a fair enough chance. Maybe Margot was right and she needed to surrender into having the kind of relationships that most people had. The kind where they loved each other, but they weren't Soulmates or some predestined epic love.

While she and Margot both knew she couldn't rock through men like Margot did, she could be a serial monogamist with a good man. Her relationship with Ben had proven that. She was positive at this point that all the fairytale books she had read as a girl were to blame for this fantasy love that had been present in her consciousness. That's why now, in her thirties she stuck to reading good ole' mysteries and biographies, with an occasional chick-lit romance here or there.

Veronica decided to text him back, although she realized she ran the risk of Bryce thinking she was a morning person. "Never seen them, but I've been listening to their music–it's really good! I'm excited to go to the show. See you then!"

It was only after she pressed send that it occurred to her that she had cut off any further communication by not asking questions or leaving the exchange more open to future texts leading up to the show. Thankfully, Bryce was not to be deterred. A minute later, her phone pinged again.

"You're going to love it. I saw them back in 2014 when they did a show with The Decemberists. Truly extraordinary. Can't wait to experience their hometown show with you."

Wow, he's really coming on strong. Or he's teaching me that this is how people pre-date, via text, her inner critic quipped.

The sun shone brightly as Veronica lay in his arms, the sheets luxuriously tangled up all around them. She still couldn't see his face, but she could feel every inch of him.

They were giggling, laughing, and playing, their bodies luminescent and glowing as they enveloped one another. Then they kissed, the sun's rays bathing their bodies as their tongues entwined and the heat between them rose.

Veronica's eyes popped open. No! Go.back.to.sleep.now. She couldn't believe how turned on she felt, almost as though she was nearing orgasm–from a *dream*. The sensations of the sun warming her skin, him caressing her in his arms, and their bodies merging was purely and utterly orgasmically Divine. And the love! The love that consumed her in every moment of the dreams–their love, their Immense Love–was overpowering.

Holy shit. This might be what real love feels like. The joy, the feeling of home, but not anything like a home I've known in this life. The etheric feeling of time and space not being relative. The perfection of our bodies. The kiss. The kissing! WOW. His tongue touching mine was like an electric circuit lighting up my entire body.

Veronica was in a daze. The dreams were happening now each day, in the early morning hours. They were so vivid and real, and yet the time in them seemed so short. She should be writing them down she thought, but their effects lingered into the day, interfering with her ability to pause and do much more than try to process what had happened. Veronica would spend the whole afternoon reliving the energy of each dream, along with the sensations of bliss and pure peace. There had to be more words to describe what she was feeling, but she couldn't place them yet.

For now, she was happy to have these dreams. And since she still couldn't see the man's face, she was left wondering if he was the man from her childhood imagination or maybe even Bryce.

CHAPTER 3

"Miss, miss, excuse me? Can you help me find a book on labyrinths please?"

Veronica snapped to attention; the kind old man's blue eyes peered into hers.

"Oh, I'm so sorry Roger, yes, of course," she said as she led him over to their mystical pilgrimages section, pulling out a book on various labyrinths located all over the world.

"Something really delicious must be happening in your life dear," Roger chuckled. "It seemed as though you were caught up in a daydream."

Veronica felt slightly embarrassed that her plight was so obvious to one of their regular customers. She nervously tucked a strand of her hair behind her ear, trying to collect herself. "Well you know better than anyone Roger, this life can be pretty magical."

"It is indeed," he said with a wink as he took the labyrinth book over to one of the well-worn leather chairs.

The concert was in a couple of days, although Veronica barely noticed. The dreams were faster in repetition now, and she spent almost every night with a faceless man who felt to her like pure delectable, scrumptious, insatiable, satisfying Love with a capital L. If he was an ice cream, she would brand him as Coconut Bliss's Chocolate Peanut Butter flavor. (Veronica had discovered she was allergic to cow dairy back in her twenties, hence the Coconut Bliss).

She started going to bed in more luxurious pajamas, like the little two-piece Valentine's pink Nordstrom number her sister had gifted her a few years ago. She rarely, if ever, wore it, but now, the dreamtime sensuality and connection was inspiring a whole new side of her to emerge. It was almost like getting ready for a spectacular date each night, only that date took place in the etheric realms. Every night Veronica would crawl into bed in a negligee or two-piece silk number, eager for their next encounter. And then, she'd wake up disappointed to find herself in her current reality without him.

She told no one about this, of course, not even her sister. Her reasoning? Veronica needed to sort out what was happening before she could let anyone in on her stranger-and-better-than-reality dreamtime activities. Was this something other people went through, too, and no one talked about it? Veronica closed her eyes, pulled down her purple polka-dotted silk eye mask, and drifted into sleep...

The scent of rose bushes filled the air while laughter echoed around them. White and gold paper streamers hung from the oak trees, and white tables and chairs decorated the outdoor park space. A white canopy covered a large buffet of food that a line of eager and joyful humans stood in wait for. Veronica's entire body hummed with ecstasy being so close to him. She was with him–outside, around other humans, on Earth! Every cell within her was turned on and lit up. They giggled together about something, although it wasn't fully clear to her what it was.

She was wearing a thigh-length aquamarine halter sundress,

her long, curly hair dropping to the middle of her back. Veronica held onto him tight, her arms wrapped around his neck, while his hands circled her waist. She looked up at him, and this time his piercing blue eyes with gold around the irises stared back into hers.

His medium brown hair was curly on top and longer but buzzed short on the sides and around the back. He had an ever so slight beard on his face which gave him the look of both an ancient Soul, yet also a young man. His light brown skin glowed with a radiance she had never seen before on Earth. He was wearing a white button-up short-sleeved shirt with tan shorts.

In that moment in the dream, time suspended. They stood like that–with people Veronica didn't recognize all around them talking, eating and going about their business–while they embraced one another, their eyes blue to green beaming into each other. It was as if in that moment, a moment they had not yet had before in the liminal space, all they could do was soak up the presence of the other, of seeing one another face-to-face in such a glorious way.

Then, in what felt both like five years later and two seconds later, time started back up again. He blinked, and a sweet, open smile formed on his lips. Veronica smiled back at him, a happiness she had not known before filling her heart. When he received her luminosity, his entire face broke into Light and he lifted it to the sky, emanating the most joy Veronica had ever witnessed from a man. That image of him was cemented into her mind as she awoke.

She sat up, gasping for air a little, as the visions of her time with him flickered through her mind, heart, body, and consciousness. It had happened! His face. She had seen his face, and it seemed so familiar. Her mind promptly went to work trying to place him. Who did she know who looked like him? She came up empty; there was no one like this man. His essence was extraordinary. Maybe even out of this world.

It was as if his name lived on the tip of her tongue. Veronica lay back down in her bed with a huff. She wished she could have more time with him. Settling into her pillow, she groaned, placing her hand to her forehead. If this dream was some kind of premonition, then Bryce was out of the running as the other half of her Soul. Bryce was fair-skinned like her and clean-shaven with strawberry-blonde hair.

But before she could go any further in processing her predicament, a knock came at the door and Margot peeked in.

"Good morning, sleepy head! Are you as excited for the concert as I am tomorrow?"

Without even waiting for a response, Margot came into Veronica's room, pulling up the blinds, letting the bright morning light in. She continued to chatter as Veronica lay tucked into her cozy, fluffy bed.

"Bryce sent me a text saying how much he's looking forward to seeing you. He just may be the one for you, sister. So get your hair done, your make-up game on and put on your favorite outfit–it's time to get you a man!"

Veronica raised her eyebrows to let her sister know she wasn't so sure about that. She sat up, peering out the window at the ocean's raucous, foamy waves, moving her body into a full stretch–all in an attempt to ignore her sister's pep talk. It didn't work and a tsk of Margot's tongue let Veronica know she was going to have to say something, anything about this dating set-up.

Looking her sister squarely in the eyes, Veronica said, "You're hilarious. And really, Margot, I would feel soooooo much better if you laid off a bit on the Bryce thing. I just don't see myself with him. He's not my type, anyway."

"Your type?! Do I have to remind you that you've dated ginger-haired men multiple times throughout your life?"

Veronica winced at the reminder and chalked it up to her Scottish and Irish heritage, "And may I remind you, dear sister, that it did not work out with any of them. Do you also remember that? It's time to try something new, don't you think? Besides, what someone looks like has nothing to do with the depth of connection you feel for them."

"Depth of connection? C'mon Ronni, let's come back to Earth please," Margot said, snapping her fingers as if to awaken her sister. "You're not going for Soulmate love here. No one gets that, remember? Except in the movies, and maybe JLo–if she's even a real human, that is."

Veronica threw a pillow at her, which was turning into a common practice, and Margot laughed, playfully slamming the door behind her. Veronica couldn't help but reflect on what Margot had said. This *was* the battle she had been in, perhaps for her whole life.

Maybe the endless love and bliss she felt in her dream state with this golden mystery man was not attainable or capable of being experienced on Earth. Maybe she *did* need to pull her head out of the clouds–quite literally–and accept a grounded, available man like Bryce. Maybe she did need to let go of her bookstore owning dream too and just get real about stepping into her forties with more going on for her than she currently had. She could always work at the bookstore on the weekends as her passion project and keep meeting up with her golden mystery man in her dream state. It wouldn't be a terrible way to live. Or would it?

The day of the concert arrived, and Veronica woke up feeling nauseous. She drug herself out of bed and attempted to soothe her tummy with organic peppermint tea and deep breaths. But nothing seemed to work. She found herself pacing the house, as if the minutes and hours were stretching into eternity. Finally after getting as ready as she was going to be, she went out onto the deck overlooking the ocean, breathing in the salt air as she stood, her hands on the railing, the ocean stretching out as far as she could see.

She had to deal with the notion that Bryce was infatuated with her and expected some kind of romantic interlude to happen between them. She had to get clear on what she thought about being officially back in the dating game. Was she ready for this? After having her heart crushed by Ben and Susie (not what she originally signed up for), this was her first official date back from heartbreak. She was starting all over again, again. At thirty-six.

They didn't even make rom-coms about thirty-six-year-olds. Society expected you to be married at least once by your forties, and Veronica couldn't even maintain one long-term romantic relationship.

But even that wasn't the most anxiety-producing part of her day. The worst part was that she didn't have a dream with her Beloved (and yes, she *was* calling him that in her head) the night before her double date with Bryce.

This caused her to spiral down into a pool of despair. What if she didn't have any more dreams with him? What if she really was going to have to show up for her waking life wholeheartedly, not in a sensual daze? Perhaps this month of dreams with her golden mystery man was some bizarro reverse psychology by her subconscious to serve as the impetus to do the damn thing and accept a reality of embracing real estate, banishing her bookstore-owning fantasy and settling (down) with a redheaded man named Bryce.

Veronica exhaled, and a raven cawed and flew by her as she did. It softened her for a moment and she imagined that it wouldn't be so bad to live a more settled, traditional life. She saw people do it all the time. She didn't have to look far to find an example of this very scenario. Her grandparents had been married for fifty-five years, and sure, they loved each other and had built a grounded and solid life together, but they weren't each other's beloveds. They were focused on taking care of their children and community. Their daily life was focused on surviving, going to church, and eking out enough money to pay for a little of life's luxuries like a T-bone steak dinner. They never were affectionate or overly expressive with one another. Theirs was a marriage of duty and obligation. It wasn't as though they were the other half of each other's Soul—and they didn't seem to mind. They had no other plans than to live and die together.

Margot was another example—she was a millionaire, selling homes. Housing sales. Nothing super Soul nourishing there, and yet people all over the world did jobs they were good at, that made them good money, that wasn't their dream job, but was good enough. Why couldn't good enough be good enough for her? What made her think she was so special that she had to live her wildest dreams (literally)?

These were the many questions she pondered as she quickly hugged Bryce when he came to pick up her, Margot, and Ryan. Bryce insisted on driving everyone, and his white BMW X5 was not only super comfy, but kind of sexy. Even Veronica, who didn't consider herself a car person, couldn't deny that. Margot was working overtime to connect with Veronica while in the car and kept making eyes at her to gauge what she was feeling. Veronica knew what she was doing and wouldn't give her more than a grin.

Veronica had surprised herself and, at the last minute, had went all out for her momentous foray back into dating. She had dressed up, wearing her large gold goddess earrings as she called them, paired with a black tank dress that fit her snugly, highlighting her ample hips, long legs, and full bosom. The black dress was the perfect complement to her black corkscrew curly hair, fair skin, and bright green eyes. She paired the outfit with some black heeled booties and a tight jean jacket to dress the ensemble down a bit. It was the Oregon Coast, after all.

When they arrived at The Starlight Theater, a buzz filled the air. The excitement of seeing The Sunshine State play for the first time in over a decade at the coast was palpable, and it seemed like all the colors were brighter and everything was glowing inside the theater.

The Starlight Theater had been renovated and was considered an ancient treasure on the Oregon Coast. Veronica's group stepped into an expansive carpeted lobby with an enormous crystal chandelier hanging overhead. A sweeping grand staircase took guests up to the mezzanine, which Veronica learned was where their VIP seats were located, giving them a perfect view of the theater.

Rich hues of velvety red, burnt orange, and cream filled the main hall, with decadent paintings of local coastal scenes featured high above. A gorgeous yellow and orange chandelier glittered in the center of the theater. The instruments for The Sunshine State were already set up with a piano, drums and guitar, ukulele, violin, and cello.

Bryce cupped his hand on the small of Veronica's back, guiding her to their seats. It was a sweet gesture and Veronica let herself relax into the beautiful scenery and prepare for the musical journey that The Sunshine State would take her on. At the very least, it would distract her from the worries on her mind and the decisions she would soon have to make.

The show opened with one of The Sunshine State's newest songs and Veronica, Margot, Bryce, and Ryan had fun bopping along to the music and sipping their wine in small plastic cups, complete with lids, of course. In the middle of the show, the lead singer introduced a song that held significant meaning to him, linked to one of his family members. Veronica thought it odd that from that song on, she saw a large golden circle or orb-type thing above the lead singer's head.

"Hey, hey, Bryce." She leaned over to speak into his ear, and he placed his hand on her leg. "Do you see that yellow circle of light up there?" She pointed towards the singer.

Bryce looked at her, his hazel-green eyes curious. "Um, no—but maybe you've had enough wine for the night?" he teased, pretending to take her cup from her.

She laughed uneasily. "Yeah, maybe, I guess."

She leaned back into her seat and now, the golden yellow

circle of light had her transfixed. How could she see this light so clearly, but Bryce could not?

"Hey, Margot, Margot!" Veronica raised her voice to get Margot's attention. She bent forward in her seat to fully get into her sister's space so that Margot could hear her. This was challenging as Margot was practically sitting on Ryan's lap while listening to the music, and throughout the show the two of them would repeatedly stand to dance and then sit back down.

"Aren't you having the bbeeessttt time?" Margot slurred a bit, indicating she may have been the one to have too much wine.

"Oh, geez Margot. Hey just look up here for me." Veronica pointed again. "Do you see a golden circle of light up there above the guy who's singing?"

Margot giggled. "Have another drink, sis!" She went back to being all over Ryan. "And by the way..." Margot leaned back in to talk loudly into Veronica's ear. "That guy singing is named Markus. Isn't he the cutest?"

Veronica tried to keep from rolling her eyes. Then she turned her attention back to what was truly important to her–figuring out whether she actually had too much wine or if there really was a golden light above that guy's head.

Maybe I am just buzzing and seeing things. Veronica tried to shift her focus back to the music.

"Hey, thank you all so much for coming out tonight and for selling out this show and spending time with us like this," the lead singer–who now, thanks to Margot, she knew to be named Markus–said. "We're gonna close out tonight with a few of our older tunes and if you know them, come down to the stage here and dance and sing along with us. We always love it when you do."

Margot let out a squeal. "We hhaaaavvveee to go down there and dance with the band!"

Good lord. Veronica glanced at Bryce and Ryan to see their thoughts on the matter.

"I've been listening to The Sunshine State for a decade man, let's get down there!" said Ryan.

While he was kind to her sister, Ryan was the typical beefy, faux-tanned, slicked-back hair pretty boy that Margot always went for. Veronica found it hard to take him too seriously. Besides, she knew her sister's pattern with men and relationships well. Margot would get excited about a guy just like Ryan, thinking he could be the "one for now" to do all the rich realtor, couple things with, and then be bored with him after a while–spanning anywhere from a few months to a year, and then start the whole cycle over again. All the while admonishing Veronica to hurry up and settle down before she was forty, an age Margot was approaching much sooner than she was. To Veronica, Ryan was just another piece of art in Margot's ever-revolving art gallery of men. She knew that Margot enjoyed the cycle of the "one for now," she merely thought it odd that Margot was so intent on Veronica finding her "forever one" so intently. In any event, it didn't exactly surprise Veronica that Ryan was game to go party down with the band at the front of the theater.

Bryce also seemed to agree, so off they went, the four of them down towards the front of the stage. While Veronica loved live music, she wasn't someone who gushed over musicians or celebrities of any kind. It was tacky and better left for groupies and Instagram influencers. Margot, however–and especially in her current inebriated state–was not going to stand idly back and subtly dance. She wanted to be as close to the band as possible, and most likely this was at least subconsciously based on getting as much attention as possible. Margot grabbed Veronica's hand and practically dragged her through the crowd to get closer to the stage, leaving the guys far behind them to catch up.

"Sorry, I'm sorry, so sorry," Veronica said as they plowed

through concertgoers to get to Margot's intended dance party spot.

She stopped about a foot from the stage, and it was then that it happened.

Veronica turned to assess her current whereabouts and right there, smack dab in front of her, was the lead singer of The Sunshine State. Wearing a light blue buttoned shirt with the sleeves rolled up, exposing his muscular forearms and paired with black jeans, he was crooning to a song she had never heard before and was hauntingly beautiful as he did. He tilted his head back, a look of sheer joy on his face as he sang the words, "cuz you're the oneeeeee."

Suddenly, for no reason, and without any conscious effort or intention on her part, a rush of tears sprung forth from Veronica's eyes. Then, a blast of energy inside her heart began radiating outside and all around her. She witnessed green light emanating from her body as it then floated into the air in front of her. Images flashed in her mind at a rapid pace of she and Markus together, of them having children, of them creating a home, of them making love, and living a life together.

The words, "I love him" formed inside her own heart. She gasped in utter shock. What was happening to her? Her mind desperately wanted to make sense of the multiple, simultaneous experiences she was having in that one moment. She was paralyzed and stuck with the very real sensation of time freezing. All that existed to Veronica now was her in a dark concert hall peering up at him, seeing him for the first time in her actual physical reality, while he sang out in delight.

That face.

His face.

The face that she couldn't quite place from her dream.

It was HIM.

The man in her wildest dreams was *this* man.

This man standing before her singing a song about The One.

This.Could.Not.Be.Happening.

Veronica's mouth was wide open as she remained rooted, unable to move, staring up at him. The tears continued to pour down her cheeks, and for the first time ever, she not only didn't care what anyone else thought, but she was rendered completely helpless to wipe the tears away.

Margot saw her tears and yelled over to her, "I know, isn't it soooo cool to see a celebrity up close?!"

Veronica blinked back at her but said nothing. Bryce finally made his way over to Veronica, placing his arm around her waist. It was that subtle but intentional gesture that activated forward movement in this scene in Veronica's life. His hands touching her body both startled her and reset her ability to move, and she finally could wipe the tears. Her mind fast-forwarded to where she was now, and the only thing she knew for sure was that she would have to process whatever had just happened some other time. Right now, life demanded that she pretend as though she were any other "fan" of a band she had never heard of before.

"Thank you again for coming out tonight, friends. We sure do appreciate it, and we sure do appreciate you. That's gonna do it for us tonight. Again, I'm Markus Mullins..."

Veronica didn't hear the names of the other two men in the band because all she could hear echoing through her Soul was Markus, Markus, Markus. She got it now. What her sister had said at their seats finally clicked into her consciousness. His name was Markus. The name of the man whom she had been spending every night with for weeks upon weeks in her dream time was Markus Mullins.

"And, hey, since this is a hometown show, we're gonna be in the lobby in about ten minutes, so please come by and say hi," Markus said in his gentle way from the microphone. "We'll be signing posters and taking photos. We'd love to see you back there."

And with that, the lights went on and the show was over.

～

Of course, the show was only just beginning for Veronica.

"Oh my God, Ronni, best concert ever, am I right?! Aren't you so happy you let me talk you into coming with us?" Margot was quite proud of herself and linked her arm with Veronica's as they all made their way back to the lobby.

"Now, I have to get one of those posters Ryan to commemorate tonight," Margot shouted up to where Ryan and Bryce walked ahead of them. "And Ronni! We can hang it up back at our place. Let's go meet these guys. They were fantastic!" Margot was exuberant, but less buzzed than earlier. The dancing had leveled her out somewhat.

"Oh, Margot, I doubt Ryan and Bryce want to wait in line to meet some musicians," Veronica said. "We can order a poster online; we don't need to get one now. I bet they even have signed posters we can order off their website."

The truth was that the last thing Veronica wanted to do was further the narrative of what was appearing to be her unwillingly playing the lead role as groupie for The Sunshine State's lead singer. She couldn't make sense as to how he was the one she had been cuddling, attending events and laughing with in the dream time. Not in her wildest dreams would she have imagined something like this could happen to her. On top of that, what did any of it mean? Why was this happening? Was Markus her Soulmate? These were all questions Veronica was ready to go home to ponder.

"I would definitely like to meet them and have them sign some stuff," Ryan said. "Maybe I should have Markus sign my chest!"

Veronica could not fathom why her sister repeatedly ended up with men like Ryan. Well, she could fathom it. After all, she and her sister had been raised by emotionally impaired humans, so of course Margot would find herself drawn to men who were not only emotionally stunted but would never satisfy her as a long-term mate. As much as Margot tried to push Veronica into being in a long-term relationship with a mediocre love, Margot was terrified of doing the same. While Margot believed Veronica could find safety in such a connection, she had no desire for it herself, and obviously Margot didn't desire it either.

Classic intimacy issues.

For Veronica, handsome only went so far, but for Margot, she could ride handsome out (both literally and figuratively) for some time. Even so, she wasn't about to ignore Ryan's embarrassing suggestion.

"Don't be silly, Ry, have them sign your wine cup or something, so you have an everlasting piece of memorabilia, duh!" Margot said, clearly irritated by his chest-signing idea.

"Yeah, I'm down to meet them and get some stuff signed too. Although I'm not interested in offering up any of my body parts." Bryce smirked over at Veronica.

Internally, Veronica grumbled. She was outnumbered and now she would further her groupie status by going to have merchandise signed by the band. She sighed. This was impossible. Her mind was filling in the blanks for this storyline before she even had a chance to reflect on what had occurred. Suddenly, she was filled with every insecurity she had tried to squash throughout her life. She wasn't beautiful enough for a famous musician. And she wasn't talented enough either. She certainly wasn't successful enough, which was obviously what someone of Markus's stature would require. On and on and her mind went, rattling off all the reasons why what had happened in the dreams and at the stage were not coherent or possible. Her heart began to pound at the thought of interacting with him and she silently prayed (for the first time ever really) that a miracle would occur so that she could get through the rest of the night without incident.

She would not be so lucky.

The four of them headed to the tables where Markus and his band would do their meet-and-greet in the lobby. But as they neared the tables, rather than a band and a mob of adoring fans, there was no one there, other than Markus. Something strange came over Veronica and she could not stop walking towards him. She became fully unaware of where Margot, Bryce, and Ryan were. It wasn't even as if she was consciously walking towards him; she was *being walked to him*. They locked eyes, his piercing blue boring into hers intently.

He raised his finger and said in his smooth Angelic voice, "Don't I know you from somewhere?"

His question startled Veronica. While she could have said, "Yeah, from the astral plane where we've been hanging out every night for weeks on end," instead she smiled slightly, tilted her head, and said, "I don't think so..."

"How did you like the show?" Markus asked.

"Oh, oh..." Veronica wasn't prepared to have direct communication with him so soon and stumbled over her words. "It was great, Markus. It was, uh, it was my first time hearing your music live and I, uh, really enjoyed it."

"Your first time? Well, I'm happy we made a good first impression."

"You have no idea," Veronica said softly, unable to break away from his gaze.

"Ronni!!!" Veronica's love haze was interrupted by the loud shriek of her sister, and by the sounds of her voice, she could guess that Margot and the boys had stopped to get more wine. "Omg, Markus! You're talking to my sister. We are such big fans. We LOOOVVEEDD the show tonight."

Markus looked directly at Veronica, and then turned to Margot, "Oh, I love hearing that, thank you so much."

"Would you please sign this poster for us? See, this is my sister, Ronni—"

"Veronica," Veronica interjected, and Markus's eyes came back to hers as he extended his hand, "Nice to meet you, Veronica. I'm Markus."

Veronica's face burned, but she maintained eye contact with him, as piercing as it was.

"So nice to meet you, Markus," she said quietly.

Margot interrupted again, clearly unable to read the room—although Veronica herself wondered if all of it was actually happening. She should pinch herself, but that would make her appear far weirder than what she was already feeling.

"Anyway, Ronni and I live together over in Depoe Bay and we'd love to hang your signed poster up in our home," Margot said, extending her hand.

"Well, that sounds lovely," Markus said, lightly shaking Margot's hand and glancing back at Veronica with a slight grin.

He either thought she was a total idiot, or he was captivated by the interaction as much as she was. Veronica noticed that time again seemed to suspend as these moments occurred between them, and of course, she secretly wished they would last forever. The energy in their brief, benign exchanges was just as coated in magic and bliss as they were in her dream state.

Markus signed the poster, and as he did, Margot made yet another request.

"Can we get our photo with you, too?"

Veronica's whole body froze in horror, as Margot seemed subconsciously intent on humiliating her in front of Markus. She was a grown woman asking a musician for a selfie! Wasn't it bad enough that they were hogging all his time, acting like a bunch of crazed groupies?

Markus was busy shaking Ryan and Bryce's hands, saying hello and didn't seem to mind the request at all.

He put his arm around Veronica while Margot was on the other side of him, taking the selfie. Bryce and Ryan were beside Veronica, everyone's arms stretched out around each other. A warm light enveloped Veronica as Markus tightened his arm around her. It was a brief moment, but it did not go unnoticed by her. All five of them beamed in front of the camera phone, and Veronica couldn't help but think how cute she and Markus looked next to each other.

"Omg Markus, thank you so much for being such a rock star–literally and figuratively tonight with the poster and photo and everything. We will always remember this night," Margot gushed before she, Ryan, and Bryce walked away. Veronica, however, wasn't ready to leave the theater lobby just yet.

Markus seemed amused by his interaction with Margot and waved. He looked over at Veronica, who was ever so slowly (i.e., not at all) backing up to follow her sister, and said, "I sure do wish there was more time for us to talk. I can't help but feel like we've met before."

Veronica nodded. "I know, I feel it too." She was stunned that he also felt something unusual between them. He was so genuine and Veronica was surprised by this as well. He wasn't the typical famous musician, and this was most definitely not the typical romantic experience for her.

"Well, if you're not too busy, message me sometime on IG and maybe we can have coffee," he said.

"I will," she replied.

He softly smiled at her and then turned to attend to the group of excited women who had encircled him.

CHAPTER 4

"Markus Mullins." Exactly one day since the concert Veronica found herself typing his name into Instagram on her three-mile barefoot beach walk. Having spent plenty of time dipping her toes in the crispy cold Pacific Ocean waters as she walked, she found a large boulder to sit on with her phone to further investigate his profile. A sea gull walked by, eyeing her strangely. Veronica made eye contact with the bird and shooed it away so she could focus on the IG task at hand.

There he was, his tousled curls, stunning blue eyes and all. Veronica took a deep breath, trying to summon the courage to honor Markus's request to reach out and message him. In the world of social media, she had heard many tales of people meeting up romantically and for business via the popular app.

I don't want to slide into his DMs. But...he did slide into my dreamtime absolutely uninvited, Veronica mused. The problem for her was that their very connection–him as a celebrity and she as a mere mortal who did not have all her shit together–went against what she believed about love and relationships. She didn't imagine herself to be the kind of woman who developed a crush on a famous musician, and then stalked him online and slid into his DMs, all with the hopes of being his next great love. He probably told lots of women to message him. And if that was the case, then she'd feel even more idiotic for doing so.

Then, there was the magic. The golden light around him, his face in her dreams, running down that mystical outdoor corridor together. Who was this man? And how could it be possible that he and Veronica had something meaningful and deep between them? Was this the Soulmate love she had longed for as a little girl? Her mind and heart battled it out, trying desperately to control something that was beyond human control and comprehension.

While she loved his dreamtime appearances, which sadly had not continued since seeing him at the concert, this new turn of events had upended her. She didn't feel much like her before-the-infamous-concert self anymore. In fact, she was so out of her body after the heart explosion situation (Veronica didn't know what else to call it) at the concert that she could barely give Bryce any of her attention. She could barely give any of the things she had been giving her attention to much energy at all since the concert.

Veronica looked down at her hands and shook them. There was a tingling, warming sensation that seemed to always be present within them ever since the concert. It was as if rays of warmth were shooting off her hands at any given moment. It was incredibly confusing to her. There was more too. She rubbed her hand on the center of her chest, as she kept feeling an opening sensation that caught her off-guard, like spirals of Light opening up inside her chest. Veronica shook her head, wondering what had happened to her.

Before she could decide what to do about reaching out to Markus, she had to get back to Margot's beach palace to have a fruit smoothie. Ever since the concert she was craving fresh fruit, fruit smoothies, and veggie juices like mad–something a week ago she would have crinkled her nose at. She had long believed the misinformation that fruit turned to sugar in the body and that it wasn't good for her. But now, all she wanted was fruit and juice, everything else that she used to eat–eggs for breakfast, salad, and fries for lunch, steak or chicken for dinner, wine at night sounded disgusting to her, and made her nauseous.

As she bounded up the boulder steps to the house, she heard a dog barking. When she looked up, a huge golden retriever came barreling toward her. She had a moment of panic, only to be replaced by joy as he came right up to her on the stairs, making direct eye contact and offering up licks and love.

She had noticed that animals were flocking to her wherever she would go, dogs and birds especially, like the sea gull and dog that had just come up to her. Every morning when she awoke, there was a blue jay outside of her window that did nothing more than look into her eyes and then fly away.

Veronica walked into the house and headed straight for the kitchen. Pulling out the blender, frozen fruit and almond milk, she became overwhelmed with the pull to listen to Markus's music. She immediately took out her phone and opened up to The Sunshine State's YouTube channel. She plugged in her speaker and let his heavenly melodies fill the kitchen. She noticed her body vibrating in unison to the beat of the music, her thighs pulsed with the music, her feet tingled and vibrated, her heart pounded in time with the beat. It made for quite the interesting smoothie making session, she thought to herself with a giggle.

This was yet another thing that was happening since the concert–she was craving Markus's music like a mad woman. It was her water in the desert, and she simply could not get enough of it. Every time she listened to one of his songs, her body would start vibrating. And she meant vibrating *everywhere*–like every place and space and crevice in her body. And so, ever since the concert, she had been stuffing her face full of fresh fruit, fruit and veggie juices, shaking her hands to make the warming sensation diminish, and listening to Markus's music while fending off a variety of birds and dogs. She shook her head, completely unclear about what in the actual f-box was happening to her.

It was as if connecting with him in the physical activated a whole other aspect of herself or her life or something, she wasn't entirely sure. She could not wrap her head around it and didn't know who she could even talk to about such things. Certainly not Margot. She would just think Veronica was crazy. She considered talking to Henry, her boss, or Meghan, who also worked at the shop, but it seemed way too out of character for her to suddenly open up to them about such personal things. She thought about perusing Books on the Beach to see if she could find a book about what was happening to her, but in truth, she didn't actually know what was happening. The only option she could think of was to talk to her oldest and dearest college friend Eloise.

Sadly, she rarely saw Eloise since she had baby number two. And ever since getting married many years ago, it was like Eloise lived in a somewhat boring (by Veronica's standards), sugar-laden Hallmark movie. It was one of those movies where the couple was so happy and in love with their two kiddos and neighborhood couples' dinners that they let their single friends of the past slip away–or endlessly tried to set them up. She knew Eloise loved her and had her back though–boring Hallmark movie life or not. So while she wasn't entirely sure Eloise would understand, it was worth a shot to tell her more about what had been happening.

~

"You met a guy?! What? When? How? Where? Tell me everything!" Eloise cozied up on the velvety chocolate brown couch at her house, offering Veronica a glass of pinot noir.

"Oh, no thanks–like I told you on the phone I just haven't

been feeling like drinking or eating much of anything other than fruit, veggies and fruit juices and smoothies. And I didn't exactly meet him in a traditional way..." Veronica trailed off. How would she ever explain this to anyone?

Granted, Eloise knew her maybe the best. They had met when they were both enrolled at Portland State University a million years ago and instantly moved in together. They were inseparable for years; partying, getting boyfriends, and then breaking up with said boyfriends, and having a blast. Now, not so much. Eloise had always been the "pretty" one of the two with her naturally huge breasts, tiny waist, straight golden blonde long hair, ever-tanned skin, blue eyes, and sweet dimples. Veronica was her wing-woman, but she felt a comfortable kinship with her that had remained, even though life's changes.

And so, even though Eloise lived in Portland, Veronica had decided that a turn of events of this magnitude was worthy of the two-hour drive from the coast to see her. She had told Henry she needed a mental health day–something she had never asked for since starting to work at the shop three months ago. He seemed unbothered by this and told her he was sending her healing vibes, which wasn't something she could recall hearing him say to her before.

Eloise's dog, a black Chihuahua mix, Sweetie, jumped up on the couch and immediately cuddled up to Veronica.

"I've never seen her do that with you," Eloise commented before Veronica could explain further. "Besides, wine is made from grapes, which you did say you were eating in volume, so it's pretty much like eating fruit." She tried again to hand Veronica the wine glass.

Veronica smiled over at her friend. Some things never changed, even though everything else in Eloise's life had. Eloise's home was now filled with Lego tables, dolls and a toy kitchen set, not to mention the screeches filtering in from the upstairs as her two children played the Memory game with her husband. Back in the day, Eloise and Veronica had spent many years drinking *all* the wine together, so it wasn't surprising that Eloise expected her to cave and drink while she hung out at her house.

"No means no El—I'm serious. The thought of wine makes me sick to my stomach right now. I can't. And yeah, Sweetie usually stays in the other room in her little dog bed when I'm around, so I don't know what's going on here, although this does seem to be trending in my life right now," Veronica said as she gently pet the precious pup, who was licking her hands.

Maybe meeting Markus was somehow making her more attractive to animals while also making her famished for fruit and his music, and activating warm healing energy from her heart and hands? If that was even a thing, Veronica grimaced. Her life was feeling a little bit out of control. She took a deep breath and began.

"Ok, so here's the deal. About a month ago I started having these really rich, blissful dreams that featured this man whose face I couldn't see."

"Ohhh...like sexy time dreams?" Eloise interjected.

"Not necessarily. There definitely have been some dream sequences where we were getting it on, but it's more like being near him is the best, most melty, most delicious, most orgasmic feeling I've ever felt in my body."

"Ooooh, okay." Eloise's brow furrowed in an attempt to understand the sensations Veronica was describing.

"So in the last dream I had of him, I finally saw his face. And he is totally gorgeous and golden and has the most beautiful face I've ever seen. I was even secretly—well now, not so secretly, referring to him as my golden mystery man. His face seemed oddly familiar, but I could not place it from anywhere. Then, I went to The Sunshine State concert at the coast with my sister, her new guy, and this guy Bryce that Margot's been trying to hook me up with—"

"Oh My God! It's Bryce! He's the guy in your dreams?!"

Veronica shook her head vigorously, laughing.

"NO. Not even close. He's a nice guy, but I had to spell it out for him via text yesterday that I'm only interested in a friendship with him, because I did meet the guy from my dreams at the concert!"

"Oh honey, this is incredible. I knew if you just gave it time, you would meet your white-picket-fence guy like my Jim."

Veronica bit her tongue. Eloise, like her sister Margot, was convinced that at some point Veronica would come to her senses and "find" her traditional love, and then they would embark on their traditional relationship complete with a white fence, minivan and two-point-five kids. Veronica had tried, hadn't she? Ben was a perfect example of this. He was a pretty traditional guy but look how that ended up? Trying to fit herself into the traditional marriage-and-kids relationship model had never felt right to her.

While Veronica didn't know all the things about Markus, she was certain he was anything but a white-picket-fence guy. He was a touring musician for crying out loud! And while Jim, Eloise's husband, was a nice guy, he also was a man who worked nine-to-five as a graphic designer for some cushy company and was in bed by 9 p.m. every night and played golf on the weekends. Veronica yawned at the very thought of it. While she supported her friend in having that kind of life, she had always wanted so much more than a white-picket-fence Hallmark movie. Or at least she thought she did.

Eloise continued. "So, who is he? When do I get to meet him? I mean, it's about time because you took it hard with Ben and I was worried you were just gonna go full-on cat-bookstore lady on us."

"Well, I *had* considered that, but my cat-bookstore-lady days may be far behind me after what has happened. So, Margot had too much to drink as she sometimes does—"

"Wait, sometimes. Is that what we're calling it now?" Eloise interjected sarcastically.

"Yeah, we'll call it that for now. Anyway, she drags me to the front of the stage during the concert, and El, there was this moment where he's singing so intently and his head is back and he's smiling and it's, it's the face of the man from my dreams!!"

Eloise gaped, disbelief filling her face.

"Oh, honey, um...you know..."

"Don't say it, I KNOW. But that's not what this is. Margot then drags us all to the back where he and the other two guys in his band are autographing stuff and he and I end up having this brief but eye contact-like-crazy conversation. He even says to me the first time he sees me, 'Don't I know you from somewhere?' He then tells me to message him and maybe we can have coffee sometime. So please don't tell me this is some kind of weird groupie celebrity crush because one, I would rather die, and two, there's something weirdly otherworldly happening here."

Eloise took a long breath and smiled at her friend lovingly, the kind of smile you give someone you think is completely off their rocker. She didn't believe her, and this stung Veronica's now very awakened heart.

"Honey, you were probably dreaming of him because you subconsciously saw his photo on all the concert promo materials. You know, the subconscious mind picks all that stuff up. And of course he was flirting with you! You're #gorgeous and I'm sure you super stood out in a crowd of old coast ladies flocking at his feet. I'm not saying he doesn't intend to have coffee with you. I'm just saying, he's a big star and you know guys like that are all about getting laid and being famous. Aaaannnddd, if you want to have a one-nighter with Markus from The Sunshine State, you know I'm so here for it. I just don't want you to get your hopes up and have him ghost you like those a-hole rock stars are known to do."

Eloise had many, many, many, if not all valid points. Points that Veronica had already considered and that her mind had tried fiercely to cling to. But something was happening to Veronica, and the way she felt in her body, well, she had never felt that way before. She didn't think Eloise would understand about the animals or the warming sensations in her heart and hands–that stuff was even too crazy for Veronica to delve too far into at this point. If Eloise thought Markus and Veronica being Soulmates was too much, she wouldn't understand anything more. Explaining it all to Eloise did help Veronica get clear–even though her friend didn't totally get it. Veronica's heart was beginning to edge out her logic-driven mind. She couldn't imagine giving up now, without at least *trying* to spend more time with him to see if there was more between them, or if it all was an unconscious fantasy.

Eloise got up and grabbed the two artfully decorated charcuterie boards she had made for their girls' night. She had been on a kick of making a variety of boards for friends and family whenever she had them over or went to a potluck. When Veronica had mentioned only eating fruit and veggies when they chatted about her coming up, Eloise decided to create a board just for Veronica. It was filled with colorful melons, grapes, apples, and orange slices along with cucumbers, carrots and grape tomatoes. She of course kept the prosciutto, Havarti cheese and Simple Mills crackers board for herself.

Eloise proudly offered the board to Veronica, sure that some food would help her gain clarity about her situation.

"Thank you El, for this beautiful fruit and veggie board! And also, for listening to me. I hear you, and I know you're only looking out for me. But I must try to at least spend some time with him to see if there's anything more between us. Otherwise, I'll always wonder. And to your point, no, I am *not* interested in a one-nighter with Markus or anyone for that matter. Maybe in my twenties I thought I could pull that ish off–I mean, you know I had that one, one-night stand, and I was horrible at it. Like so awkward and…"

Wrapping a piece of prosciutto around a slice of cheese, Eloise began cracking up, "Oh yeah, that's right. You didn't even know how to have a one-nighter! You were asking the dude about it, like how does this work. You're hilarious! But maybe now as a sexy cougar in your late thirties, you wanna give it another go?"

Veronica laughed so hard; Sweetie looked up at her sideways.

"You're scaring Sweetie Ronni? Knock it off!" Eloise teased.

"I have absolutely zero plans to turn into a hot cougar, although I do think Markus is a couple of years younger than I am, so I mean, maybe..." Veronica teased back.

"Okay, so did you message him then?"

"I couldn't do it," Veronica confessed. "I found him on Instagram, but you know I hate that shit. I meet my partners like normal humans do, on an online dating site. Or at a bar or event or work or a friend sets us up. Sliding into his DMs is a tough one for me, even if it's by request. Anyway, he has so many 'followers' I don't even know if he would see my DM...I don't know if I can do it."

"Well, if you want to see if there's truly a connection there, you're gonna have to humble yourself and then get over yourself. My friend Marcia slid into the DMs of her now husband, Brent. There is no shame in that game, girl. Besides, you have nothing to lose at this point."

Except my heart. Veronica sighed to herself.

"Markus Mullins—Follow."

The button glared back at Veronica.

A new customer walked into the bookstore and Veronica quickly clicked out of her Instagram account and refocused her attention.

"Hello, welcome in! How can I help you today?"

The older woman smiled brightly, a kindness emanating from her face. "Do you have any of the Markus Zusak books here?" she asked.

Markus. Right, of course.

"You know I think we do," Veronica said as she got up from behind the oak desk and escorted the woman to their fiction section to show her one of Markus's books.

It was one of the many things she loved about working at the bookstore. It was not only the perfect cozy cabin size, but rather than having computers for customers to look up titles, she and Henry and the other woman who worked at the shop, Meghan, would take customers to titles and assist them in finding what they needed.

Sometimes customers would come in and say, "Take me to your favorite romance novel. That's what I want to read next." And whoever was working that day would take them to it. Books on the Beach was also well-known for carrying quirky metaphysical books and they'd have readers from all over the state coming to them for obscure and random titles like *2150*. Usually, if someone was searching for it, they either carried it or could hunt it down which meant that sometimes they had used titles also available for purchase.

It was a warm, personalized experience and allowed them to form a special book-lovers community that was unique to the Oregon Coast. The Oregon Coast itself notoriously attracted introverts, writers, artists, and other mystical beings. Books on the Beach was attuned to this and served its community well. It was something Veronica hadn't fully understood when she took the job a few months ago, but she was steadily growing to love the quirkiness and the bespoke service they provided.

After helping the old woman find her Markus book, Veronica went back to the tall oak desk. She suddenly realized that the music that normally played softly in the background was turned off for some reason. While they usually played Coffeehouse Café from Sirius radio in the store, sometimes they would play the local coast 102.7 Kyte FM radio station. She could have sworn she had it on that morning, she thought. But she shrugged, and turned-on Coffeehouse Café (her favorite), sitting back down to go through the weekly book order.

"If you're the one, then I'm the one. If we can be one, let's be one."

Veronica's head jolted upright to attention. Markus's song, well, The Sunshine State's song, "The One" was playing. WTF. She had never heard that song on Coffeehouse Café, at least she didn't think so. She hadn't known about Markus's music until the concert.

Just then the door opened and the UPS driver entered with a delivery, his name badge proudly displaying his name– "Marcus."

"Have a delivery for Henry Goodwin," he said.

"Yes, that's the owner, I'll sign for it," Veronica said as she stared at the man's lapel. "Thanks so much, Marcus," she said, half-smiling, half in shock, her heart pounding a bit more loudly in her chest.

The old woman came back with a few books to purchase, including the one by the Markus author she had asked about earlier. "You know dear, I've been a voracious reader my whole life. Here I am, nearing eighty and I still can't stop reading as many books as possible. I got myself a perfect pair of readers and I do my Tibetan eye chart and you know what? My eyes hold just fine with it."

Veronica chuckled, the conversation soothing her. "I love that," she said as she leaned in. "And I plan on being the same way when I get to be as glorious as you are. By the way, what's a Tibetan eye chart?"

"Oh, look it up dear on that Internet or something, you can print it out. It's an ancient eye exercise and it really strengthens your eyes. I only use my readers occasionally now because of it."

Veronica wrote it down on her little notepad. "Duly noted. I will check it out. Because I, like you have a reading habit that must be sustained for as long as possible."

"To the death!" the woman said with a wink. "If there is death, that is."

With that, she ambled out of the store.

Veronica scratched her head, not sure exactly who the sweet old woman was or what she meant by whether or not there really was death, but their exchange delighted her all the same. She had also given Veronica a few things to ponder. How wasn't death real? And did she also need to use a Tibetan eye chart? She made a note on her notepad. She was sure they had a book about both topics somewhere.

The bells dangling from the entrance door chimed again, and a woman and her son entered the bookstore. Immediately, the boy went running at top speed towards the children's section, "Markus, please no running in the store, honey!" the mother shouted out after him, throwing a quick apologetic smile in Veronica's direction.

Markus.

He was freakin everywhere right now.

It was as if there was some strange conspiracy happening in Veronica's life that was scheming to keep Markus in front of her. She sat back in her chair, chewing on her lip. Was the Universe trying to tell her to stop delaying and follow Markus on Instagram? Was that it?

Well, okay then. Don't work so hard Universe, I'm on it. She pulled open an Internet window on her phone, typed in Tibetan Eye Chart on her Ecosia search, and then opened another window, and pulled up Markus Mullins on Instagram. She hit "Follow" and then immediately closed the window and put her phone in the top desk drawer.

"Okay, that's done then, isn't it?" she said out loud to no one in particular.

Ping.

Her phone.

She pulled it out to see that Markus Mullins had indeed accepted her follow request in record time.

Butterfly sensations filled Veronica's chest and stomach, and her hands pulsed with warmth. She put her hand on her stomach reflexively and heard the same whisper she had heard before at the concert. Only this time, it was much louder. "I love him."

This whole thing was getting so strange, so weird and so ... magical. Veronica couldn't help but feel herself coming alive and wanting more.

Just then she got another ping from her phone. Markus had messaged her. Her whole body seemed to fill with excitement, turn-on and light at the very moment she saw his message come through.

"Hey Veronica! It was lovely to meet you the other night after the show. I've noticed thoughts of you popping in since then. How about getting that cup of coffee soon? I have a couple of tour stops to do and then I'll be back at the coast next week. My number is 503.777.1232. I'm better at texting, so reach out that way and we can talk further. Have a great day! -M"

Veronica reread the message several times, attempting to tease out the full intention behind it. It was a tad flirty with his mention of having thoughts of her, but otherwise it was neutrally friendly she decided. Now, she would need to text him a reply. Did she want to do that right away, or should she give it more time?

As she pondered the question at hand, Henry walked into the store, his face sweaty, looking as though he'd ran a few miles or jogged to the store itself.

"Hey, what are you doing here? You're supposed to have a day off, remember?" Veronica said.

"A day off. What are you talking about?" Henry joked. "Actually, I'm here to see you. I got a message for you this morning in my meditation."

Veronica was mildly aware that Henry meditated regularly and had a strong spiritual life, thus his penchant for stocking ancient wisdom and metaphysical books in his shop. She hadn't asked him too much about it in the few months she had worked there, although she certainly respected whatever his beliefs were.

Veronica had gleaned bits of information about who the real Henry was based on the books she saw him reading or recommending to customers. She found she could do this with most anyone. Want to know what's *really* going on with someone? Find out what books are on their nightstand or their go-to book recommend and you'll learn a lot.

Veronica noticed that Henry almost exclusively read or recommended mystical books such as *Many Lives, Many Masters, The Alchemist* (and anything by Paulo Coelho really except for his more recent books, which Henry had deemed lacking in the high-vibrational spiritual frequency that encompassed his earlier work), and books like *The Celestine Prophecy,* along with some more obscure authors with mystical titles. From the small quips she overheard him making with customers and Meghan about past lives, energy bodies, and his energy medicine healing sessions, she would have classified him as being fully woo. They had even talked about bringing in a tarot reader or psychic to the bookstore as a community event, and Henry had been working to find the perfect match. He didn't want any quacks, only legitimately gifted healers as he put it. Veronica found herself fascinated by all of this, and even now she could feel a tug at her heart towards investigating it further.

"A message in your meditation for me? Since when are you getting Divine, spiritual messages in your meditations, dear sir?" Veronica asked.

"Since always, but you never asked, so I haven't gotten too far into it with you. *And* by the looks of things my dear, you're being catapulted into a spiritual awakening right now, so you're not only going to need these messages, but I also have a feeling we'll be talking about this kind of thing a lot more."

Veronica noticed something in Henry's face she had never seen before as he stood there before her. He was ... he was smirking. Yep, that's what that look on his face was, a smirk. From the brief conversations Veronica had overheard, Henry had been married twice and loved going to the gym, especially for the sauna. He was fascinated by the mystical and had referred to believing in a Divine Counterpart, who would come to him at the aligned time. These were all things Veronica took in at the time as being tidbits about who Henry was, it was certainly not something she ever considered would be part of her experience.

"Excuse me? A spiritual awakening? And are you smirking at me? You're enjoying this, aren't you? Well if you must know it appears that I've been plunged into some kind of weird, seemingly mystical experience and it now appears as if the whole Universe is talking to me, but I'm not understanding what it means exactly."

Henry appeared positively delighted. "This is perfect, absolutely perfect. I have been waiting for this day. Soon, we'll have a whole bookstore of enlightened employees," he said playfully motioning his arms in a grand fashion, although Veronica could tell he was also serious. "So, would you like your message then?"

"Um, yes, please. I think," Veronica grinned.

"Okay, well," Henry glanced around the store, noticing the mother and her son Markus still in the children's section, snuggled up on one of the couches reading a book together. He lowered his voice, "So you're having a kundalini awakening of True Love with your Holy Beloved, otherwise known as your Divine Counterpart. The man you met, I wasn't shown who he was, only that you had been having dreams about him and then met the very man you had been dreaming about in person. He is incredibly important to you, so you want to follow all the signs that point to him. You may notice random things happening, like his name showing up everywhere and strange 'coincidences.'" Henry used his fingers to denote italics.

"Yes, that's EXACTLY what's been happening. Henry, you're psychic? How did I not know this? I'm going to have to sit down for this honestly," Veronica said, as she stumbled back into the tall stool that sat at the main checkout desk.

Henry seemed slightly offended that she hadn't noticed earlier. "First of all, everyone is psychic once they start consciously working with their advanced body technology, and second, I've been meditating daily since 2002, so, of course, I'm psychic. That's also why it's so important to me that if we bring a reader into the shop, that it's someone legit."

"Well, clearly, we could have you do the readings, Henry. There's no reason to find someone else. But...back to me," Veronica laughed nervously. "It's plain bananas that you would have received all that information about me. Wait a minute...is that because I'm your employee?"

Henry's attention was suddenly distracted as he appeared to be busy lining up the books next to the main desk area.

He cast a quick look at her, more seriously. "All in due time dear Veronica. But are you noticing new body sensations and other oddities?"

Veronica was watching him closely; she was having trouble believing how cuckoo her life was getting. "Yeah, I've been having bizarre warming sensations coming from my palms and heart, and also dogs seem to really like me now where before they stayed far, far away, and also these blue jays keep coming to my window every morning and birds come to me on the beach too." As she said this, she remembered on her way into the store yesterday, a man's dog practically knocked his owner over to get some affection from her.

Henry nodded in affirmation as she spoke, and then said quite matter-of-factly, "Yes, animals and babies will start flocking to you, that's another thing that happens once your first spiritual awakening occurs. Your aura is glowing and all with the eyes to See come running. You'll also notice looking at the clock at unusual times, like 3:33 or 12:12p. This all indicates that you're in the midst of a spiritual awakening. This is wonderful Veronica, isn't it just wonderful?"

CHAPTER 5

Veronica wasn't sure how wonderful it all was, but clearly something mystifying was happening to her. Whether it was a spiritual awakening as Henry believed, or some kind of spell she fell under when she agreed to attend that concert, she didn't know. What Veronica *did* know was that she needed to text Markus Mullins, the famous multi-talented musician, about having coffee together.

She agonized far more than she needed to about sending that text. She must have written a half dozen versions sitting at the cherrywood kitchen table overlooking the roaring Pacific Ocean, before she finally, out of sheer frustration, was going to send, "Hey, it's V, let's meet up next Friday at 11 a.m." She couldn't sort out how friendly or flirty or aloof to be–in fact, nothing she wrote felt right. Mid-agonizing Margot waltzed into the kitchen.

"Whatcha doin' sis?" Margot asked as she grabbed an apple from the fridge. "From all the huffing and puffing I heard, it sounds like you're stressing over something?"

Margot had an exasperating habit of calling out her observations about Veronica in a sing-song-y, critical way.

Which was both infuriating and, in this case, mildly illuminating.

Veronica cowered, dropping her head onto the table. "Oh nothing, just sending a text, and yes, thank you for noticing. I AM agonizing about the right thing to say."

"Let me give you a tip then, sister. I can tell you haven't read that book I gave you, btws, so I'll give you some CliffsNotes now. The energy you have when you write a text, email, or anything, really, is embedded into whatever you're creating. So if you're annoyed or agitated while writing that text, that energy will come through to your recipient. Best go for a walk, or here, try out one of these superfoods shakes to shift your mood before sending that text."

Margot grabbed her pink Birkin bag off the counter and pulled out a silvery package that said "Purium USDA Organic PowerShake" and set it on the kitchen table in front of Veronica.

When she stared at her quizzically, Margot shrugged and said, "My assistant started taking these organic superfoods from this company, Purium, and seeing you struggling like this I had a hunch you might benefit from it. She did a ninety-day cleanse with them and lost like thirty pounds, and she's radiant since she started with this stuff. She has more energy than I've ever seen, she's sleeping better than ever, it's pretty mind-blowing. She gave me this bag to try out the PowerShake, but since I'm already perfect. . ." She smiled coyly before continuing. "And you're only eating fruit and smoothies these days anyways, I thought you might want to try it out. Apparently, it has the nutritional value of six organic salads or something. So, why don't you put five tablespoons of this in the blender with organic almond milk and some frozen organic berries, drink it, *and then* send that text. Okay?"

Margot sauntered out of the kitchen, shimmying her bum and giggling. Veronica put her hand to forehead, laughing in return. Sometimes she thought her sister was sent to aggravate her, but at times like these, she was convinced her sis was an Angel, sent by whoever was running the show on Earth to help her out.

What Margot shared about the energy transfer made sense. She could see that the energy one holds when creating something can transfer to those who receive the creation. And since her smoothie routine could use a change, Veronica decided to follow her big sister's advice. She grabbed the bag to make herself a PowerShake.

❀

Okay, I can do this. The PowerShake was not only delicious, but it also seemed to clear Veronica's anxiety and brain fog so she could send the damn text already.

"Hey, Markus! Thanks for the IG message. I Love Salt coffee shop–wanna meet there? Let me know what might work for you. Btw, you've been showing up in my dreams–it's been wild! See you soon, XV"

Veronica pressed send and set down her phone.

There. That's it. *Thank you, PowerShake. I just needed to shift my energy; Margot was right. Perhaps I should read that* Life of Magic *oracle book she gave me too...*

Whether or not Henry was right about her having a spiritual awakening, something important *was* clearly happening; she was communicating with Markus Mullins after all! Veronica had to keep digging deeper into it even if it all seemed confusing. She couldn't keep brushing off the coincidences in her life, calling them weird, and then walking away. Henry had suggested she meditate daily, claiming this was the most powerful spiritual practice that would allow her to connect to her higher self. He had invited her to a group meditation that he hosted weekly at his house.

She figured she might as well try it out.

"Place your hand on your navel, and your other hand on your heart, and take a nice, deep breath," said Henry.

Five people were gathered in his living room in a circle, Veronica included, preparing to meditate. Henry was sitting at the front of the room in an overstuffed white armchair with a camel throw and pillow. A man sat comfortably cross-legged on a cushion to the left of him with another woman sitting on the leather couch across from Veronica. Meghan, a young woman in her late twenties with ebony dreadlocks and big brown eyes, who also worked at the bookstore, although usually on Veronica's days off, was laying down on the taupe shag area rug on the floor.

Veronica wasn't sure what her best meditation pose was, so for now, she was leaning up against Henry's leather couch opposite from where the older woman and man sat, with a pillow under her bum. She hadn't quite known what to wear either, but she figured black leggings and a purple hoodie would do with her hair pulled back halfway, her curls loosely tossed to one side.

Candles glowed from the white brick mantle, maple coffee table and end tables, while ambient harp music played softly in the background. Veronica had never been to Henry's house before, but loved how inviting and simple it was. The style reminded her of how he had decorated Books on the Beach. Taking a big breath, she attempted to focus on Henry's voice and nothing else.

"Now breathe in through your nose and out through your mouth three times. Each time, imagine that you're gathering up the contents from the day and then exhaling them out, releasing what no longer serves you."

Veronica imagined she was inhaling the angst she felt waiting to hear back from Markus, as well as her angst about not having any more dreams with him. Her nights seemed lonelier somehow when she woke up, realizing she hadn't spent the nighttime with him.

She also inhaled her growing restlessness about her work. Veronica had always imagined herself owning a bookstore by now, with a bookstore cat or two, weekly events, bestselling author signings, and a position in the community that revered the literary art form. But with no substantial money in savings, her paychecks going toward a room in her big sister's house, and an old Toyota 4Runner as her primary transport, her dream had drifted further away than ever. And as Margot so blatantly pointed out, she would be forty in four years—was this what she wanted at the potential halfway point of her life?

All of this immediately came to the forefront as she sat down to meditate. Was it supposed to be like this? Veronica followed Henry's guidance and kept gathering up her penetratingly anxious thoughts and then releasing them with every breath.

"Continue to work with this breath. We'll do this for thirty-three minutes," Henry said.

Veronica internally bristled. Her first meditation would be thirty-three minutes long? That seemed like forever for someone merely starting a meditation practice. How was she going to get through it?

Henry continued, "I'll come in throughout the meditation to remind you to return to your breath. Whatever thoughts present, continue to gather them up with your inhale through your nose and then release them by exhaling out of your mouth."

After about ten minutes, Veronica noticed a lightness in her body, so she breathed into that to activate it further. Then she felt him. Markus. She felt him enveloping her, almost as if he were hugging her energetically. She had never experienced his delicious energy so potently in a non-sleep state. She breathed into this and further activated it as she did.

Veronica was floating in a state of no time, simply being

present with the sensations of lightness and Markus all around her. When Henry's little bell chimed to end the meditation, she came to a start, shocked that the thirty-three minutes had breezed by so quickly. As she opened her eyes, she noticed that the room seemed brighter and more luminous. She felt grounded and at peace.

So this was why people meditated. It was truly rejuvenating, not to mention magical, and this was only her first time. Suddenly, she had an intense craving for another PowerShake and couldn't wait to get home to make one.

Henry then went around the room, asking each meditator to share their experience. Meghan sat up from her position laying on the floor and began tapping her head, and then heart and stomach in a strange fashion Veronica had never seen, before sharing her experience, "I came in upset. My parents and I have been fighting a lot lately as they don't approve of me and my Holy Beloved, and I felt so unsettled and shaken by our argument. But about midway through the meditation, it all lifted and I was filled with an expansive love for them. I finally felt free of the anxiety."

Henry seemed to identify with her experience. "Beautiful Meghan, it's not uncommon for healings to occur during meditations, especially group meditations. It's why I practice daily and why I recommend it to everyone I can." He grinned at Veronica. "It's the single most powerful way to heal yourself and stay connected to who you really are."

Edward, a fit bald man in his sixties dressed in a stylish navy cardigan and linen pants, chimed in from his cushion near the couch, "Yes, I've been meditating daily for twenty years and I completely echo what Henry shared. It's my ride or die practice if you will. No matter what's happening in my life, I meditate. And I find when I meditate in groups like we did tonight, my healing *is* accelerated. I have greater releases and increased peace and clarity. Would you agree with that as well, Henry?"

"Absolutely," Henry confirmed. "That's why I love hosting

this weekly meditation. It sort of ramps up our individual, daily solo practice."

"Okay, so I have a question..." Veronica surprised herself by interrupting. She had planned to stay quiet since this was her first time meditating and she didn't know what she was doing.

"Yes, Veronica, do ask. I can't promise I can answer it, but I'll do my best to try," said Henry.

"Alright, well, I'm new to all of this. I recently started having a series of dreams that led me to meet this person, which then led to all of these seeming coincidences that Henry tells me are really synchronicities. I'm having all this energy come out of my hands and heart, and animals are running up to me everywhere I go, so Henry suggested I try this. It was honestly amazing. I feel almost like a new version of myself stepped forward from this one meditation alone. Which is cool, but slightly peculiar. Anyway, so, my question is, what does a solo meditation practice look like? How do I carry this into my day-to-day life?" It startled Veronica that she was revealing so much, but she did feel like another, elevated version of herself after that meditation. She felt more open, vulnerable, and softer, yet more vibrant. It was hard for her to comprehend with her mind, but she felt it fully in her body.

Everyone was smiling at Veronica as she spoke, their warmth emanating towards her.

Henry stretched out his legs from his chair and replied, "Fantastic question Veronica. This is one I can answer. Simply, every single day, set your timer for thirty-three minutes to meditate. Thirty-three is a holy number, symbolizing pure love. I've found that meditating for this length of time allows you to connect more deeply with The Divine inside of you and around you. Put on some ambient music if you'd like, or sit silently if you'd like, and do what we did here today. Focus on your breathing. Inhale through the nose and exhale out of the mouth. Gather up whatever comes in that doesn't feel lit up and as though it serves you, and exhale to release it. At some point, as it sounds like you've already found, you may enter a state of peace and calm. Then, you'll ride that wave for as long as it lasts, and return to the breathing with the gathering and releasing focus if thoughts or worries come in. Try it out this week and then next week join us again for our group meditation and you can share what you noticed. Sound good?"

It sounded easy enough, and Veronica felt excitement tingle through her body. Would she have the same results alone? Would Markus's presence be made known to her again as it had today? Edward had said that doing the meditation in a group accelerated those kinds of things, so she wasn't sure what she might uncover in her own daily practice.

"That sounds doable. Thank you so much, Henry. I do have one more question, and I suppose it's for the group, too. I noticed that someone I have a deep–maybe even what you could call Soul connection with–showed up while I was meditating. Is this common? Is this something that happens?"

A woman in her late sixties, Cecilia spoke up. Dressed in an off the shoulder red tunic and flowing black pants, she smoothed back her gorgeous, wavy red mane, her many copper and gold bracelets jingling as she answered, "Well, if he's your Holy Beloved, then yes, that can happen."

"My Holy Beloved?" Veronica repeated, slightly stunned.

"Yes, ancient tradition has it that there's a select gathering of Angels who incarnated onto Earth and they incarnated in pairs. Their mission in every lifetime was to find each other, return to one another and then create more Love and Light on Earth through their union."

Cecilia leaned in, her green eyes earnest. "Finding each other wouldn't be too hard to do either, because they always incarnate fairly close to one another, ensuring they'll always meet up in every lifetime. So this connection with the Holy Beloved is rooted in the ones who carry it and takes place at an infinite energetic and spiritual level. Meaning that they'll come to you in your dreams as you've already experienced, they'll show up in your meditations, and you'll see or hear their name everywhere. Many report that the Holy Beloved comes to you energetically before physically. It's a powerful phenomenon that many Angelics experience."

Veronica stared at the wonderful woman before her in awe. She had summed up Veronica's experience over the past few weeks perfectly, although she wasn't so clear on what qualified someone as an Angelic. The others seemed captivated by what Cecilia shared as well, only the flames of the candles flickering could be heard now as they all breathed in the wisdom she had conveyed. And then Cecilia continued.

"If an Angelic does not yet know they're an Angelic, the meeting of their Holy Beloved or what some call their Divine Counterpart will throw them into a spiritual awakening of sorts, filled with synchronicities and mystical experiences. So dear Veronica, if this is what you're experiencing right now, my advice to you is to go with it. Follow every coincidence, every sign, and keep saying yes to your Beloved. Because the caveat to all of this is that the negative energies here on Earth do not want the Angelics to unite with the other half of their Soul, and so blockages will be put in each individual's Way."

"What kind of blockages?" Veronica blurted out, adjusting herself on the pillow she had been sitting on and moving it behind her back. She already had enough fears about these bizarre circumstances. She didn't want to worry about blockages, too.

"Blockages such as not getting support from friends or loved ones for the union, like what Meghan is experiencing with her Divine Counterpart, Eric. Blockages like traffic, technology, or other strange mishaps that lead to missed calls/texts/meetups. Blockages like random sequences of events that delay or stall your meeting and cause odd miscommunications. You can also find the negative forces speaking through your friends and loved ones, discouraging you from the union and from a life together. And worst of all, blockages like the whispers in your mind that say you're not worthy of the union, or that you'll never be together in this lifetime."

"Your own thoughts? How could those be blockages?" Veronica asked, perplexed, unsure as to how this could be possible.

Henry looked over at Cecilia and she nodded. There seemed to be some kind of telepathic communication happening between them.

"Veronica, a lot of what you think you're thinking isn't even yours. Instead, your 'thoughts' are programs that live within the artificial matrix on Earth. Programs of unworthiness or programs that say you're supposed to get married, work a job you don't love, have a bunch of kids and a mortgage, and one vacation a year. It's not that there's anything wrong with those things on their own. It's only that it's not actually what every Soul came to experience or even wants to experience. And it's certainly not the peak of what life on Earth can deliver. When you hear negative thoughts whispering in your mind, it may be some of these programs."

"Or..." Henry looked at Cecilia and the others leaned in more closely. "Or it may be the negative agenda energies trying to throw you off the path of your destiny."

This was getting to be too much for Veronica. "Henry, you can't really believe this. Like mists of energy sneaking into your mind to tell you not to bother with your Beloved?"

"That's exactly right," Cecilia said. "It's more like a snake-like energy if you were to see it energetically, and it sadly directs a lot of human behavior. I've spent decades working as an energy healer and I've seen these energies myself—we all have in our various meditation and healing experiences. But it doesn't have to run you if you're aware and refuse to believe the lies it tells you. And that's why I say that those thoughts in your head, which aren't even yours, can be the biggest blockage. So be mindful of this, Veronica, and do not succumb to it."

"Veronica," Henry interjected, his voice lowering and

growing in seriousness. "We believe you are an Angelic, as are all of us here. I know this may seem like a lot for you right now, but with your recent awakening and your experience in tonight's meditation, it's imperative that we all tell you the truth about what's going on here. As an Angelic you have a highly important assignment and mission on Earth. We've been patiently awaiting the day that your awakening would begin, and we want you to know that we're all here for you as you navigate this new terrain."

Henry was correct. This new information officially put Veronica into overload mode.

"You believe I'm an Angelic?? You all are Angelics?? You've been waiting for me to awaken? What the actual frick, Henry?" Veronica stood up, dizziness sweeping over her as her legs wobbled underneath her. "I'm a messed up human being just like everyone else. Nothing more."

Edward, the man who had spoken to her earlier, stood up in front of her. "Is that why ever since you were a little girl you had this feeling that you had a Soulmate here on Earth? Is that why you were drawn to having a bookstore your whole life? A bookstore that would draw you to Henry and to all of us, who are part of your Angelic spiritual family?"

"Wait—you mean, you think that we've all known each other before we were humans?"

"Yes, Veronica, yes. You'll start to remember us more and more as time goes on. Don't give up now," the younger woman Meghan said from her seat on the floor.

"You know about all of this too, Meghan?!" Veronica asked, the adrenaline in her body surging. Part of her wanted to leave immediately, while something within tugged at her to stay.

"Yes, I remembered when I was seventeen that I was an Angelic and started feeling the call to my Holy Beloved," she said, her eyes sparkling as she spoke, gold teardrop earrings hanging from her ears and a gold Ankh necklace dangling low over her teal crewneck sweatshirt and leggings. "I began having mystical experiences like seeing auras and what you might classify as 'dead' people. I had been living in northeast Portland, going to a high school I hated, and working at a Nike retail outlet on the weekends. My parents were too self-involved with work and their own dramas to even notice what I was going through. And then, around the time I graduated high school, I started having dreams about a bookstore at the beach where my spiritual family was. At first, I assumed it was from a past life, but I kept having the same dream again and again until one day I heard a voice say to me, 'Go to Newport! The bookstore and your Angelic family are there!' That was nine years ago, and that's even why I work at the bookstore today. When I found the shop, it looked like what I had seen in my dreams, and Henry was super familiar to me, too. I began meditating daily, and not long after, I met my Holy Beloved Divine Counterpart Eric. And that's how the journey began for me."

Veronica was enchanted as Meghan shared her story. She shook her head in disbelief as she imagined that Books on the Beach had an otherworldly magnetic pull and power to it that called in its Angelic family. Her mind said it was all crazy, but something about it felt familiar too.

"Soooo...is this like an intervention, then? An Angelic intervention?" she said. "And don't Angels have special powers and abilities like what Meghan has experienced? I mean, guys, I don't think I qualify–I don't have anything like that!"

Henry tried to hold back his laughter, as Veronica lowered herself onto his brown leather couch.

"It's not meant to feel like an intervention, Veronica. We're merely excited for you to remember. Didn't you ever wonder why you got the job at the bookstore? I had over a hundred applications and you had a spotty employment history jumping from bookstore to bookstore every ten months or so in the city with no previous metaphysical book experience. But still, you got the job, at a really solid wage for retail no less." His hazel eyes twinkled.

"I mean, I *did* notice that and I did wonder how I got such a good bookstore gig as they usually only pay minimum wage. I'm used to having to work two jobs to cover basic expenses. But I could not have imagined it was because I had a spiritual family and that my desire for a bookstore was linked to guiding me to them. How did you know who I was?" Veronica asked, her voice shaking.

"I had a dream, of course," Henry said as he grabbed a mug of tea from the end table near his chair and took a sip. "I was shown a young woman with black corkscrew curls and fair skin with freckles and emerald eyes. I was shown that you were the next member of our spiritual family that would be coming in. I had been shown a few decades earlier that my assignment was to bring my spiritual family together and create a safe space for them. I was also to mentor them–gently, of course, through the process of their awakening."

Cecilia chimed in, "Over time, and as you come together with your Holy Beloved, Veronica, more clarity will come to you about other members of our spiritual family that you're here to assist. You may choose to do this more obviously in the Earth matrix as a healer or spiritual guide as myself and Edward do, or you may do so as Henry has chosen, more under the radar."

"Yeah, Henry totally could have opened a psychic shop or something more obvious," said Meghan.

"Why didn't you, Henry?" asked Veronica.

"Would you have cozied up in a psychic shop? I mean, I know Cecilia and Edward might have. But Meghan and Veronica, would you have applied to work at one even? Would your Holy Beloveds or other members of our spiritual family be found hanging out there?" Henry surveyed the five now brightly shining faces.

Edward and Cecilia laughed, and Meghan and Veronica shook their heads no. Veronica thought he was right. If Books on the Beach hadn't been the only bookstore on the Oregon

Coast, she might have been more inclined to work at a store that resembled the other bookshops she had worked at before. Reflecting back on her interview with Henry she realized he had downplayed the metaphysical element, most likely in an attempt not to scare her off. As she listened to Meghan, Cecilia, Edward and Henry, her body relaxed and she had the distinct feeling of being held by some force she didn't quite understand.

Henry continued. "That's why I didn't do it that way. I knew that the Angels I was here to assist would not have been naturally drawn to anything other than a warm and Light-filled bookstore. By the ocean, no less. We're all drawn to the ocean as it naturally cleanses our energy fields and keeps us connected to our spiritual family in non-physical. That's why sunsets are so important to attend as well–they're the perfect time for us as Angels to give thanks for the day and to receive a clearing from the negative ions emanating from the ocean. And so, long story long, that's why I created Books on the Beach. Besides, I've also had numerous lifetimes as a writer and scribe, so it fits my energetic profile far better than anything else."

Veronica was now completely speechless. Her mouth gaped open as she saw her entire lifetime click into place. This was why she never felt like the other kids at school. Why she always felt somehow a little different and separate. She had tried to have a party phase and even a promiscuous phase–because that's what you do on Earth when you're young, right? Only it didn't take for her. It all felt so wrong. That must be one of the programs in the matrix that Henry was speaking of that kept Angels and human Souls off their destined path.

No wonder she couldn't shake her dream of the bookstore; it was leading her to Henry and her spiritual family. It was why Ben had to cheat and break up with her, which sent her running from her beloved Portland to the Coast to nurse her heart. She had given up her dream of being with her Soulmate so long ago because of those whispers in her mind that told her it wasn't reasonable. And Margot too! Margot was always telling her to get over that dream and find a nice man to settle down with and a job that would make her a lot of money...Oh no. Margot.

"Oh, my God! My sister. She sometimes gives me the worst advice regarding following my dreams or deepest desires. And sometimes she brings me the best resources and advice. What does that mean, that she's part of these negative agenda energies?" Veronica's pulse raced and terror ripped through her.

Henry scanned the room and it seemed the group agreed he should answer this question for her.

"It could be, but it's more than likely that the snake-like negative agenda energies are merely whispering to her those things and she's regurgitating it to you. Sometimes close family and friends turn out to be entities associated with the negative agenda, but it's rare. As Angelics, we rarely set ourselves up with direct entity energy like that, although it's not impossible."

Her parents. Past partners, bosses, and co-workers. Even her past therapists. How many times had Veronica made decisions throughout her life based on advice they gave to her? And who were they? And who was influencing them? Veronica was viewing everything differently.

"How many of us are there on Earth right now?" she asked the group.

Cecilia answered, "We don't have a clear confirmation on specific numbers, but it's believed that there are 144,000 of us incarnated at this time."

"144,000 total? So, 72,000 couples?"

"Roughly, that's believed to be the case. Others believe there are 222,222 of us, or 111,111 couples. I prefer the latter as the numbers seem more Angelically magical, but you know the Bible prophesied 144,000 as did other spiritual texts, so that number tends to take precedence."

Edward injected, "The exact numbers don't really matter. What we know is that in a world of reportedly eight billion people, there are few of us here. But there are enough of us to have a positive impact and more of us here than any other time on Earth. A special configuration of us was summoned by Source long ago so that we could be here for this time. And you see, one Angelic couple united in pure Love can positively affect 22,222 Souls. This allows the Earth to reach the needed 22 percent tipping point for it to shift back to a place of Love so that it's no longer a place of suffering. The agreement made with the hijacked agenda was 22 percent, and if we all can unite with our Divine Counterparts, and shine the Light of our creations, this can easily happen. Our alignment with Source and with our Divine Counterpart amplifies our impact and means that we have more positive Angelic energies at our backs than the rest of the world. We incarnated in groups, so like we are all in a group, there are many small groups of Angelics located all over the Earth."

Veronica suddenly noticed that Edward and Cecilia were sitting very close to one another now. A pink hue of energy surrounded them too, something she had never seen before. They seemed to notice her noticing them and Cecilia spoke up, "Yes, we're Holy Beloved Divine Counterparts. We found each other over a decade ago while we were both married to other people and had teenage children. We quickly let our existing partners and family know what had happened and moved forward together. Then, in our meditations, we were guided to move to the Oregon Coast to meet the rest of our spiritual family. And that's when we found Henry."

The day those dreams began, Veronica's life was forever changed. And now, with these revelations, she was certain she would never be the same again.

CHAPTER 6

Veronica slid into the peanut butter leather driver's seat of her white Toyota 4Runner in a daze. Her mind could not fully process all that she had just learned at Henry's. The center of her chest was pulsing with what felt like Light ever since Cecilia started explaining what Angelics were along with their path on Earth. Her palms were warm, as though spirals of energy swirled within them. Instinctively, she released a deep breath to shift the energy and then had the impulse to pull out her phone from the console where she had left it during the meditation. A text from Markus awaited her. It had come through when she was meditating. How down-to-the-minute was it to when she began feeling his presence?

Veronica let her 4Runner run while leaning her head on the headrest, immersed in thought. She could no longer ignore the fact that after a month of this strange turn of events, she felt more like her true self than ever before. After almost a month of fruit, juices, smoothies, and now PowerShakes, she was also feeling better in her body than she had since she was a teenager. She waved to Cecilia and Edward as they backed out of Henry's driveway in their silver Bronco and drove off.

Veronica noticed that she had more energy; she was sleeping

better and she couldn't help but admire her figure. At 5'5 she had a thicker build, only now she was noticing a new glow from her skin and she felt leaner and more toned than she had in years. She had more energy and overall optimism about the future too–something she had struggled with throughout her life. She had always felt so different from others, and now . . . now she was feeling a new sense of belonging.

It seemed impossible that she was an Angelic and that Henry, Edward, Cecilia, Meghan and maybe even others she hadn't met yet were part of her spiritual family. But her heart, her palms, and the synchronicity taking place in her life all seemed to indicate that it was true. And now, she was starting to believe that it *may* be her truth. She wasn't a hundred percent certain because her mind (or were those the programmed thoughts from the negative forces?) kept signaling that the whole thing was pure banana-cakes. She was sure that anyone she dared to share this information with would claim it was nuts, but her heart and Soul said, "Yes, this. Yes, this is The Way!"

"Would love to meet you at Salt, it's one of my favorites too. How about next Friday, at 2 p.m.?" Markus's text read.

How had she and Markus never seen each other at Salt in the past? Although with his touring schedule and celebrity status, perhaps he snuck in through the back and sat huddled up in a corner. She wondered about Markus's relationship with his celebrity status. Was he fully identified with it? Did he see being famous as integral to who he was or merely a fun byproduct of living his mission? Was he grounded and humble? Did he have a line of women in every touring city, or was he more of a relationship guy? She had hesitated to read anything more about him online because she wanted to know the real him, and that meant also seeing what the energy was like between them when it was them, together.

Veronica's cheeks heated. The prospect of being alone with him, of being close to him, of being an "us" with him, lit up her entire body and stirred parts of her that had never been touched before. Could this actually be her path?

She waved once more as Meghan's blue Prius drove past her, leaving Veronica as the only car parked in front of Henry's house. She sighed and put her 4Runner into drive, to make her way home.

I must have done something right in my past lifetimes, if I even truly believe that I had them, to have Markus Mullins as my Holy Beloved.

∽

I can't believe I thought Markus Mullins was my Holy Beloved Divine Counterpart! Veronica lamented as she waited at Salt, perched on the sapphire blue sofa, eyeing every customer who entered.

It was 2:22 p.m., and he wasn't coming. She was sure of that now. She exhaled, looking down at her black heels, high-waisted denim jeans, and purple, three-quarter-sleeve, scoop neck top. She had tried on a few outfits before deciding on this one for her first meet-up with Markus, pairing it with huge gold hoops, her hair down, lightly tousled, and parted on the side.

Now a perfectly fantastic outfit had been wasted on being stood up. She strode to the counter and ordered a brownie and a toffee cookie. Salt was fashioned as a boutique café, featuring local artists and makers, and also stocked with a full gluten-free and traditional menu of quiches, soups, coffees and teas, kombucha, and sandwiches.

She would eat her emotions today, with gluten and sugar, instead of bursting into tears at the café. She hadn't realized how invested she was in this meeting with Markus. And with him ghosting her like this, all her feelings of unworthiness and beliefs that Soulmate love would not and could not work out for her came rushing in.

Who do you think you are? That someone like Markus would want to be with you?!

Markus Mullins is not going to fall in love with some bookstore clerk who lives with her sister at thirty-six. Get over yourself!

In what world does a talented musician end up being your Holy Beloved Divine Counterpart? Do you really believe that you live in some magical world where you have a Beloved, and are part of a Soul family of Angels on Earth, to help humanity? Wake up, stupid!

These were the thoughts traipsing through Veronica's head as she sat stuffing her emotions on that sapphire couch, no longer eyeing the customers who walked through the door. Instead, she put her full focus on inhaling her brownie, cookie and white chocolate mocha. She hadn't bothered to message Markus to follow up, and he hadn't messaged her, so she would let the whole thing go. He clearly wasn't someone who followed through, or even bothered to cancel if he couldn't make an appointment. *Must be a celebrity thing.*

She groaned, remembering how she had gloatingly told both Eloise and Margot about their coffee date this morning and how she was sure they had a special bond. She had video chatted with Eloise briefly who was proud of her for finally reaching out to Markus, but still remained skeptical. She had briefly mentioned to Margot in passing this morning that she had a hot coffee date with a certain rockstar they had just met. Margot had shockingly been more concerned for her sister's heart than overjoyed at the possibility of a hook-up with a famous musician. In fact, both Eloise and Margot had smiled and nodded, attempting to be supportive of her, but she could see they thought she was a straight cray-pot for thinking that Markus Mullins would be anything more to her than a fantasy. She wouldn't be able to face them; not yet anyway.

It was all too good to be true. *Me, an Angel here on a Divine Mission, with a sweet Angelic family to support me, united with*

*my Beloved, carrying out our work to assist humans at this time—
oh, V, what were you thinking?*

The voices in her head seemed unrelenting, taking every
opportunity to beat out of her any notion of her lovability or
that she was an Angelic, or that Markus was her Holy Beloved
Divine Counterpart.

It was now 2:44 p.m. and Veronica could not justify
staying at Salt any longer. All the hope had drained from her.
The worst part was, she couldn't call up Eloise and Margot to
vent about being stood up. She couldn't carry on about what a
jerk he was and how unfair his ghosting her was. The two
closest people in her life had expected this to happen. They
expected Markus to ghost her at some point, showing his true
colors as an elitist, entitled musician. Second, they would only
use this occurrence to encourage her to join the rest of
humanity like they had done to live a more socially accepted
life. And maybe they were right. As she walked back to her car
in the bright Coast sunshine, she thought that perhaps it was
time to grow up, take a job as a realtor, and give Bryce another
chance.

Just then, her phone pinged. Her heart leapt with the
possibility that it was Markus. Unfortunately, that wasn't the
case. It was Cecilia. She and Edward were having a spontaneous
dinner at her house with Henry and Meghan, and Meghan's
Holy Beloved, whom Veronica hadn't met yet. Would she like
to pick up some things for an organic salad, maybe bring some
PowerShake (they all wanted to try it after hearing her rave
reviews), and join them?

While Veronica didn't feel like socializing, she knew she
couldn't go home to Margot's questions about her coffee date.
It would be better if she spent more time out until she could
formulate a plan of what to tell her.

After replying to Cecilia's text, she headed to Trillium
Natural Foods, the local health food store. Fortunately,
Veronica had some PowerShake with her in the car that she

could share. Once parked at the health food store, she promptly deleted Markus's phone number from her phone.

This too shall pass, Veronica said to herself as got out of the car to pick up the veggies for the salad. She had used this phrase repeatedly during the Ben break-up. It had helped her tremendously then, but so far it wasn't helping now.

Markus Mullins walked into Salt at 3 p.m., curious about what his connection with Veronica truly was. She had overpowered his thoughts since that night at the concert, and he couldn't shake the feeling that he knew her from somewhere, although he couldn't place where or how. He was used to meeting attractive women at shows, media appearances, and other events. But at thirty-four, he was craving something deeper than what he had experienced before. A twelve-year relationship with his college sweetheart had wounded him terribly, but that was more than three years over with and he was starting to feel ready to lean into love again.

"Hey, Markus! So good to see you," Lili, one of the employees at Salt greeted him as he approached the main counter, passing the paintings, jewelry, and kitchenware that Salt featured.

"Yeah, hey, good to see you too, Lili. I'm meeting someone here but you all are looking pretty cleared out right now." Markus said as he surveyed the café.

"Oh yeah, we close at 3 p.m., but I'm happy to get you a drink to go before we do," Lili said.

Panic struck Markus as he realized a huge mistake had been made. His business manager, Katie, handled the scheduling of his appointments. Since she lived in LA where the record label was located, they met via Zoom every week, during which he would have her add any personal meetings to his shared calendar, and she would review his touring, record label, and other commitments with him. Either she had written it down improperly or he had somehow given her the wrong date and time.

It didn't matter now. Veronica obviously would have thought he had blown her off. But she hadn't texted him earlier to see where he was. Maybe today wasn't even the day they were supposed to meet? Markus pulled out his phone to scroll through his texts with Veronica to confirm. Sure enough, he saw that he and V had agreed to meet at 2 p.m., not 3 p.m. at Salt.

"Hey, Lili, thank you for the drink offer. I'll take a decaf oat milk latte, and I'm also wondering, did you happen to see a woman in here waiting around the past hour? Curly black hair, freckles, bright green eyes?" Markus asked, glancing up from his phone.

Lili smiled. "Well, she sounds beautiful, Markus, as I'd expect for you, but no, no, I don't recall seeing her here. But we've been busy today, so perhaps I missed her."

Markus was disappointed but thanked her for her help and sat down to wait for his coffee. He always loved the sapphire blue couch at Salt. It had a vintage feel and dramatic design that fit perfectly with the camel suede couch across from it and the cream armchairs tucked throughout the space around the merch tables and displays.

Perhaps Veronica had met someone else this past week and blew off their date. Maybe the Universe was protecting him, like it was known to do. Markus had always considered himself lucky and perhaps it was his imagination coupled with his strong desire for an authentic connection with another human that caused him to project that onto Veronica. She wasn't like most women that chased him, she was grounded, real and was devoid of desperation. Perhaps that freshness had him misinterpreting their connection.

Markus felt like a fool. Even though he seemed confident on the outside, he was awkward when it came to romance. He seemed to naturally choose the wrong women. They were either women who needed to be rescued, or who wanted the benefits of his success, fame, and money. But ever since he was a little boy, he had this feeling that there was a sacred and special union for him to experience in this life. He had believed that perhaps Noelle was that person for him when they met in college, but it had devolved into a toxic push-pull relationship that resulted in her sleeping with his good friend, a fellow musician.

Maybe he had been wrong about Veronica, too. If she had cared where he was, Veronica would have checked in with him. After all, he could have had a good excuse for being late. He would leave it and trust that if they were meant to connect further, she would reach out. A small voice inside of Markus pointed out that it was he who had gotten the time wrong, so perhaps the most integrous action would be to follow-up with her and apologize for that.

But there's no proof that she even showed up for the date, so what's the point? I'll just look like an even bigger fool if I reach out to someone who may not even be interested in me.

"MM!" Lili called out from the coffee bar.

Markus stood up, grabbed his decaf latte, and made his way back to his car, a red Tesla, and drove himself down the 101 North to his house overlooking the Tillamook bay.

As Veronica drove the 101 South to Cecilia and Edward's home, tears poured down her face. Not only did her "this too shall pass" mantra *not* work, but she also couldn't believe she had bought into the notion that Markus was the man from her dreamtime and that they belonged together. Nor could Veronica believe she could feel so miserable as she drove down the epically gorgeous coastline that laid out before her.

The views were beyond striking as huge rocks and crags lined the 101, and the ocean and its frothing waves lapped gently against the rocks. Along the way, beach access points were available and Veronica loved stopping at different pull-outs to discover new views and walks. Today, though, she would bypass them all, hoping her tears would dry by the time she got to Edward and Cecilia's with the veggies from the store and her bag of PowerShake. She didn't know how she was going to break it to everyone that she wasn't who they thought she was, but she would have to find a way.

～

"Veronica!! We're so happy you could make it on such short notice!" Edward cheered as he opened the door to his and Cecilia's two-story, wood-shingled beach home in Newport's Nye Beach. Two four-foot statues of Angelic beings stood at the entrance to bless and protect the house.

"You have no idea how perfect your timing was in sending that text." Tears filled Veronica's eyes as she stepped into their light-drenched home. Before her was an expansive living room with walls painted in buttercream, adorned with artwork featuring an assortment of artists' renditions of angels. The living room spilled into the dining room and kitchen area.

Edward immediately noticed her tears as he helped her bring in the bag of groceries.

"Cecilia, Cecilia dear, get your sage," Edward called as he and Veronica walked into the large l-shaped kitchen where Cecilia, Henry, Meghan, and another man were gathered around the white and blue tiled island, sipping kombucha on ice from stemless crystal wine glasses.

The minute Veronica saw them all, she burst into tears. Meghan ran over and hugged her.

"Oh, honey, I'm so sorry. But whatever it is, we'll sort it all out," she whispered to Veronica.

"Thank you," Veronica said, completely unable to control the tears that flowed from her eyes. She had tried her best to

87

stuff her tears before pulling up to Cecilia and Edward's home, but obviously her best had not sufficed. She didn't know how she would tell these kind and open-hearted people that she wasn't who they thought or how she would eek out the embarrassing story that Markus had stood her up.

Everyone gathered around Veronica, and she soon smelled the wafting fragrance of sage.

Meghan held a large bundle of sage and was moving it all around Veronica's body and energy field. "White sage was known by the Native Americans to be a powerful clearing and cleansing agent, with the ability to clear negative thoughts, energies, entities, and other unhelpful attachments from humans, animals, and spaces. This sage is clearing you now for your highest peace, joy and of course, clarity."

"Whenever you're ready, love, feel free to tell us what's troubling you," said Cecilia.

Veronica released her tight grip on Meghan's hand and was instantly handed tissues by Meghan's Holy Beloved.

"Hi, I'm sorry you're meeting me like this. I'm Veronica," she sniffled.

"No worries at all, I'm Eric, Meghan's Holy Beloved. I'm sorry for whatever is hurting you so," he said.

Eric was the most harmonious match for Meghan energetically. Veronica could see their energy bodies so perfectly merged. Eric was tall with dark blonde hair and gleaming blue-grey eyes. The two, side by side, standing in front of her was a sight to behold. They simply fit together, much like Cecilia and Edward.

"Oh my Goddess, you two are such a perfect match!" Veronica exclaimed, witnessing them in front of her.

Everyone erupted into laughter.

"That's the way of the Holy Beloved," Cecilia crooned as she made her way back to stir a big pot of delicious-smelling sauce in the kitchen. Cecilia's wavy locks were piled on top of her head, her signature gold bangles jingling from her arms, and an array of gemstones decorated her fingers and ear lobes. She was dressed in jeans, with a silky turquoise blouse and a grey apron. She was barefoot as was Edward and the rest of the Angelics. Standing next to each other, Cecilia and Edward had a glow around them in a way that was one unified energy field. It was breathtaking to witness, and a bit much for Veronica's tender heart at the moment.

Veronica burst back into tears again. "I think you all have me mistaken. I'm no Angelic and I definitely don't have a Holy Beloved Divine Counterpart. Markus and I were supposed to meet for coffee today and he ghosted me. He never sent a text, he never showed up, nothing."

Veronica was in full ugly cry-sob mode now. Her mind was utterly shocked that she would let a room full of people who were practically strangers, including her boss, see her like this. She buried her face in her hands and shook her head wildly. "I'm so, so sorry you all thought I was someone I'm not. Clearly, I'm not an Angelic. Just look at me. I even ate my feelings today instead of meditating and finding a healthy way to deal with the overwhelming sensations that I'm a total and complete loser who will never experience true love."

Henry came over and stood in front of Veronica. She knew it was him even with her hands over her face, simply from the presence of the energy he carried. He stood there silently until she was done sobbing and finally looked up. When she did, he handed her another pile of tissues and said, "Veronica, have you been having these thoughts since Markus didn't show up for your date that say you could never have a love like this and what's wrong with you for believing in yourself as an Angelic or in him as your Holy Beloved?"

Veronica nodded.

"Are you certain those are your thoughts?" he asked.

Suddenly, she remembered what Cecelia had warned her about. Cecelia beamed at her encouragingly. A light came on inside of Veronica, and almost instantly, the tears that had flowed from her with such abandon dried up.

"Oh shit. I didn't even catch that! As soon as he didn't show and it was clear he wouldn't, I immediately went and got some sugary treats for myself as well as a coffee, and all these negative thoughts started pouring in. Thoughts that said this was all crazy and that I should go back to living like everyone else seems to live on Earth."

She looked around and everyone nodded in understanding. Veronica was not alone; they had all experienced something similar on their journeys as well.

"That's how it works," Edward said. "The refined sugar and caffeine is toxic to your system. Its manmade and it lowers your frequency. Once that happens, the negative agenda energies can more easefully insert the lower-vibrating thoughtforms into your field. If you have any sense of unworthiness, which most humans have from childhood trauma or other traumas and programming in the matrix, it's incredibly easy for these nonsensical thoughtforms to activate in your mind. If you believe them as true, which most humans do, you'll go back to living the way the artificial matrix encourages everyone to live, disconnected from your true origins and mission, and thus, you'll never fulfill your destiny. All of us have faced these very same challenges Veronica, it's part of the path of becoming who you really are. In your case, and in the case of all of us, we're Angels."

Suddenly Veronica could see it all so crystal-clearly. Like she could literally SEE what she had just gone through. She saw the playback of her sitting at Salt, the realization he wasn't coming, the whisper placed in her ear to have some sugary and caffeinated treats to make herself "feel better." Then she saw herself inhaling the sugary cookie, brownie, and latte. As she swallowed each piece, it lowered her vibration further and further. Finally, she saw wisps of energy encircle her, whispering in her ears, and she saw her wounded little girl in her heart, absorbing it all and believing it.

"Ohmygod. I cannot believe I couldn't even access the memory of Cecilia warning me about this as a possibility. It was as if I had never had that conversation with her before, even though clearly Cecilia, you psychically knew that I would have this experience, and soon."

Henry spoke up, grabbing his glass of kombucha and ushering Veronica to sit at the long table in the dining area with Eric and Meghan, while Cecilia and Edward listened in from the kitchen. "We've all had these experiences as Edward shared, Veronica. Even now, we all have to be mindful of not getting sucked into family drama or collective drama, otherwise, we open ourselves up to infiltration. And once you're in a lower-vibrating state of fear, unworthiness, sadness, and despair, your higher brain function is offline. There's no way for you to access the Divine Guidance that wants to flow to you that would show you something entirely different about the situation."

"This is why doing daily self-healing around limiting beliefs, fears, and traumas is so important," Meghan added. "I used to self-sabotage any love that came into my life, or any good that came to me. The minute something didn't go the way I thought it should, I would do exactly what you did. I would eat fast food or sugar-laden foods, or drink a bunch of wine, or I would binge-watch some low-vibrating series on Netflix. And then, I would be susceptible to the negative agenda messages that would tell me not to bother or try and to instead settle for the life that everyone else seemed to be living–a mediocre, grinding hustle towards death."

Veronica laughed out loud. "It *is* a mediocre, grinding hustle towards death that we're all programmed to believe is life on Earth, isn't it? Work a job you hate, toil for dollars, and not even enough dollars to do too much with. Get into debt and have some kids that btws, cost millions of dollars to support. Then, you celebrate a variety of holidays that cost tons of money and are laden with unhealthy foods. From there, humans are consistently fearful, eat toxic food on the regular, get poisoned with 'medicines' from the mainstream–I mean, it's absurd when you really start to look at it!"

"And the entire time humans are avoiding consciously acknowledging the reality that their physical day-to-day life won't go on forever," said Henry. "They're avoiding that every moment they spend doing things they hate, with toxic people, eating toxic foods, in relationship with those who aren't their Beloved, living a life disconnected from nature and The Divine–they will painfully, despairingly regret it all on their death bed. They'll wish back every moment that they spent out of alignment with The Divine and they'll wish for more time doing what they love, with people who love and adore them, in union with their Beloved, in harmony with the Earth."

Veronica noticed Edward and Cecilia hugging in the kitchen, kissing gently while Meghan's head now rested on Eric's shoulder. A peace filled Veronica, as she began to innerstand her personal journey and the journey of humanity more clearly from everything that was being shared with her.

Henry continued, "This is the trap that Earth can ensnare humans into. It's why it's so important that we don't live in that way, that we don't give in to those negative, self-defeating thoughts, and that we instead stay true to our heart, that we heal our wounded parts and beliefs and we live as an emanation of what a Divinely connected human looks like on Earth. So you not doing what your sister or friends or society say you should do, Veronica, is yet another sign of who you *really* are. An Angelic, here to shine the Light so that as many humans as possible can awaken to their true Divine nature and return to unity with themselves, The Divine, and the Earth."

Tears once again filled Veronica's eyes. This time not from sadness or a victim story of being rejected by Markus Mullins. But from her Soul shining through her body. Her Soul was saying YES to the truth that Henry spoke over her. She raised her left arm in front of her, the hairs standing at attention, and chills flooded her body. Waves of energy cascaded from her crown down to her spine.

She knew who she was.

And she was a freakin Angelic–with or without Markus Mullins.

CHAPTER 7

"Hey, Katie, it's, Markus. Do you have time to talk now?"

Markus shuffled his feet, holding his cell phone in front of him with Katie on speaker. He walked slowly through his backyard, which in the summer was filled with ripe crabapple trees and featured a picnic table with string lights overhead. His jaw clenched. This conversation was a long-time coming.

Markus's business manager of many years, Katie McMahon, a spry woman in her early fifties who always wore her shoulder-length brown hair back in a tight bun, paired with her signature pencil skirt and fitted jacket of various monotone shades. Clearing her throat, she responded in her sweetest, most candy-cane tone.

"Oh hey Markus, yes, of course I have time to talk to one of my favorite singer-songwriters in the whole entire world. I do have another call on the line, though. Can you wait for a minute while I wrap it up?"

Markus did his best not to audibly gag. While Katie had been his business manager for years, there were moments like this when he wondered why that was the case. She had come highly recommended by his label as being one of the best in the business, with a long history of assisting artists with managing touring, events, and music production schedules.

Occasionally–throughout the many years she had been assisting him and the band–he wondered if she was intentionally working *against* him. This scheduling mix-up with Veronica added yet another pit in his stomach about Katie, and if he was being honest, about his long-time record label. He was sure he had told her to block out his whole day for a special meeting with V.

Instead, his schedule had been adjusted to show the meeting at 3 p.m. along with another meeting with label executives added in at 5 p.m. His gut instinct suggested this was more than a random mistake. As frustration moved through his veins, fear also took hold. Was he willing to let go of his label and the way he had been making money for over a decade? Was now the time to sever the ties that had given him a life of fame, social acceptance and clout? He wasn't sure, but he did know today's conversation had to happen.

"Sure Katie, I'll wait," he said.

Katie quickly shushed the record label conference room and its guests, and shifted her focus to Markus's agitated state. After deferring him for a moment, Katie put the call on hold and immediately began shouting at the two men in the room.

"It's Markus, and he sounds *very* displeased with our little 'adjustment' to his schedule, gentleman. I'm going to have to up my game on acting as though I've lowered my IQ and cannot make simple scheduling adjustments. That way, he'll calm down and you two can direct him appropriately for his next album."

The two men looked at one another in a self congratulatory manner.

"We're always grateful for your service to our artists Katie, you know that," said Mr. Schwan, one of the men sitting at the head of a long, black conference table. "You are brilliant at handling Markus and helping to guide him to the decisions that ultimately serve his career, the label, and, of course, the messages *we* want out in the world through his music."

Mr. Schwan was a difficult man to look at. At allegedly eighty years of age, he was grossly overweight, although impeccably dressed. He notoriously wore wire-rimmed glasses and was mostly bald save for the ten or so strands of hair he carefully placed over the top of his head. His grotesque appearance did nothing to affect his status and power, however. Schwan had been running the mainstream music industry practically since its inception and now worked as a consultant to all the various major record labels.

He worked closely with government officials to shape the messages and music that were released on radio and via streaming stations everywhere. He also worked with industry executives to oversee the relationships that mainstream celebrities engaged in. It wasn't uncommon for him and his team to gather with movie executives to choose the next actor and musician combination that would drive the collective wild with obsession and envy. Markus Mullins had been identified as having quite a large impact on the collective consciousness with his lyrics and melodies, not to mention his striking good looks. Schwan and his team had big plans to bring in more subliminal messaging to his music to help control the population into greater states of submission with governmental agendas.

Sitting with Schwan was Mr. Newton, the reigning president of the record label. In his late fifties, Newton's attractiveness almost made him look plastic, his bright-white veneered smile, faux tan, tailored suits, and slicked-back salt and pepper hair screamed wealth and power, which happened to be two of his favorite things. He was known to be ruthless in his tactics with artists and within the industry. Newton and

Schwan were close companions and considered themselves a power duo in the industry.

"It's important that Markus only have special meetings and relationships with industry-approved females, as we've shared with you before, Katie. Especially after all we did to break up his long-time relationship with Noelle," said Newton, who awkwardly scratched the back of his head, a green scale momentarily visible. "When you told us about Markus's schedule change that included this woman V, we did some digging and realized that was not the aligned match for Markus. By making that scheduling adjustment, as you call it, you were serving the best interest of not only Markus, but you could say of the collective consciousness. It's important that Markus is paired with another celebrity of similar status and that they convey the kind of relationship that humans will be endlessly desirous of and will chase rabidly. Of course, this will be futile, because this kind of relationship doesn't exist, anyway."

Katie's expression remained unchanged, listening to them both mansplain to her what she had known throughout her twenty years of working in the music industry. Everything that went out into the mainstream public was heavily controlled–music, movies, celebrity relationships, tragic events, etc. Markus was simply another spoke in their wheel of control and manipulation. He, like every other artist Katie had ever worked with, came to them wide-eyed and fresh, intent on being as famous as he could be. Unfortunately, though, he did not realize, just like all the others, how much of his Soul he would have to sell for that to happen.

Katie had noticed a difference in Markus lately, though. He seemed more distant and less interested in his fame, including keeping it alive at all costs as he had been before. She wondered if this V character was part of the reason for this, and judging by the reactions of Schwan and Newton, she posed a considerable threat to their plan for Markus's impact upon the collective.

"Are we now ready to be quiet, gentleman, so that I may do

my job with Markus as you've directed?" she said, smoothing her bun and straightening her skirt.

Both men gave a nod indicating that she may proceed. She cleared her throat yet again summoning her sweetest vocal tone and took her call with Markus off hold.

"Markus love, are you there? Hi, I'm back. So sorry about that, we had a delivery go awry, and I was managing more than a few people to get everything back on track. Now, what can I help you with?"

"Katie, it's happened again and I'm angry, as you no doubt can tell. I am certain that I told you that today I had an important meeting with V and to block off the rest of the day from other appointments. Can you tell me what's going on? You know this has happened on several occasions, especially it seems when I have private, personal appointments to attend to."

Katie took a breath to pause, as if reflecting on Markus's observation. "You know Markus, I'm sooooo sorry about that. I'm not sure how that happened. Maybe Mercury is in Retrograde again or something?" She shrugged. "Anyway, I'm so sorry you missed your special meeting, *but* it is incredibly important that you're on the call with Mr. Schwan and Mr. Newton this evening, and it's now 5:20 p.m., so you've already kept them waiting. You're in luck though because they're both sitting right here with me now, so why don't I put you on speaker so we can have this meeting?"

"Katie, listen," Markus said, adrenaline running through him. "I know that while I pay you, you're ultimately at the behest of the record label, primarily those two men sitting in the room with you now. I know that there are conversations that happen between you and them about me that I'm not privy to. I'm frustrated by this. And it would make me a lot more comfortable if I could at least feel, even momentarily, like you were an ally of mine. Instead, it's starting to feel like I need to be managing you as opposed to the other way around."

While Markus didn't consciously intend to come across so bluntly, his anger and built-up resentment over the years of working with Katie and the label were coming to a head. Over the years, he had experienced creative differences with the label, and often he had the feeling that Katie was merely a handler who was manipulating him to work in harmony with the label, even when it was not aligned with his true intentions. Because he had started the band and wrote all the music, he was the one who interacted with the label. His two bandmates were happy to show up for concerts and interviews, play their instruments, sing back-up and let Markus handle the rest. Markus had gone along with a lot of it because truth be told; he wanted to be famous and successful in his musical career. He swept aside the small voice within him that whispered that something was off with Katie and with the record label. They got results for big-name artists, and that's what he wanted too. So he stuffed his intuitive knowing and did as Katie and the team directed.

Sometimes the label had detailed requests about the content of his songs and about who he was in a relationship with–whether that was romantically or as friends or musical partners. He had wanted to tour with a little-known but off-the-charts talented artist, Adam Singer. Adam wasn't in support of the mainstream power systems and his music reflected this as it was written sincerely from his heart. He questioned authority, and the large corporate entities that were running the entertainment, healthcare and government industries. Markus loved this about him and supported him in using his music as an outlet for sharing his political and spiritual beliefs. But when he lobbied hard to have Adam open for The Sunshine State's last world tour, the label had been incredulous and refused to support the pair in touring.

Katie had been, as usual, on the surface, supportive of what

Markus wanted, but he couldn't shake the feeling that her positive "support" was merely a façade. Ultimately, she was steering him to conclude that having Adam as the opening act was too risky for The Sunshine State's reputation. Markus hated that he had caved to the pressure, and he despised even more that he cared about fame and having the "right numbers" on the music charts and in his bank account as much as he did.

"No one gets this famous without caring about those things," he begrudgingly muttered to himself.

"Ooh, okay Markus, well, thank you for all that you shared. I promise you this won't happen again. Now, do I have your permission to put you on speaker so we can honor your appointment with Mr. Schwan and Mr. Newton?"

Markus would never have agreed to have a meeting booked after his time with Veronica, and he was certain he had told Katie to block out the rest of his day. He had no idea what the executives wanted to meet about, but he was curious if it was to discuss the contents of a recent song he wrote and recorded with the band, inspired by his friend and fellow singer-songwriter, Adam. He took a shuddering breath wondering if he had the courage to move on from the label, or if staying for a few more years, just to get to the next level, would be best.

"Go ahead and put me on speaker, Katie. But I hope you'll take what I said seriously," Markus said as he walked towards the back of his house and turned on the overhead lights, creating the ambiance he needed for this important call.

Katie pursed her lips in response and put the call on speaker. Markus tensed as he heard her announcement that Mr. Schwan and Mr. Newton were also on the call, unsure of what to expect.

"Markus, your last album has been doing incredibly well on the charts for some time now, and we'd love to see you take your career to the next level," said Mr. Schwan.

"I'm listening," Markus replied, trying to be as present as possible.

"Think Best New Album Grammy, invites to every industry event, hob-nobbing with your music idols, think Music Hall of Fame Markus," added Mr. Newton, his voice growing more enthusiastic.

Markus was shocked by the turn of the conversation. "You're not concerned with the demos I've made for the next album, that's not what this is about?" he asked.

"Oh, not at all Markus. We love your creativity, and of course, there will be some tweaks once we start recording in the studio. But before we get to any of that, there's some prep work that needs to happen," said Newton.

"In order for us to help you reach the new heights of fame and impact, Markus, there are some more things we need from you," said Mr. Schwan. "There's a certain actress, Isabel Alvarez, that we think would be a nice pairing for you at this time. You and Isabel dating would do a lot to further both of your careers and get more eyes and attention on you. We'd like you and Isabel to start being photographed together in the next month, which would support her upcoming movie launch and start to build anticipation for The Sunshine State's next album."

Markus was silent, feeling uncomfortable with this intrusion into his personal life. He had made the mistake of taking Schwan and Newton up on an offer like this once before, and it was now coming back to haunt him. He had never expected that his personal and professional life would be so controlled by the music industry duo.

"You know we'll have all the best producers working on your band's next album, Markus. You have that legacy-level star quality, and we only want to help you achieve that," said Newton.

Markus finally found the courage to speak. "I've greatly appreciated your support and help with my music career over the years. But interfering in my private life is starting to make me uncomfortable."

"Interference?! Markus, who said anything about that? You

know you always have free will to decide! You humans are so ungrateful. You know if you don't like what we propose, we can take it all away from you and you'll be back to who you were before, a big nothing!" Schwan's voice grew louder and louder, and Markus could feel a thick, inky energy emanating from him through the phone.

Newton tried to calm the situation. "Markus, we could never make you do anything you didn't want to do, of course. But we can point you in the right direction, and when you follow what we outline for you, you'll see huge shifts in your career. Look at all the success you've already experienced by letting us direct you. However, the choice is always yours. So why don't you look up Isabel on social media, see what you think, and let Katie know when you'd like an introduction made between the two of you? We can have photographers catch you two out together after that."

Markus felt muddled as he ended the call. The prospect of Grammy's, Music Hall of Fame, and legacy-level wealth and impact were everything he had ever wanted.

He put his head in his hands as he sat on the picnic table, groaning inside. Anything more with Veronica wouldn't be possible now. Was it worth it? Was a Grammy worth letting her go for good?

Markus wasn't sure.

"So, what do you think you're going to do next about Markus?" Eric asked as he passed Veronica sea salt for the delicious homemade meal they were enjoying at Cecilia and Edward's long oak dining room table. Veronica swallowed a bite of organic gluten-free fusilla bathed in a rich veggie pasta sauce, and promptly dug her fork into her plate for another bite.

She admired how Cecilia and Edward had decorated their home. It was filled with prayer flags and statues of great masters such as the Buddha and Jesus Christ, along with Mary Magdalene. The dining table alone could seat up to ten and had two long benches with colorful silk cushions and two single benches at the head and foot of the table. Out of the window, they could see the ocean stretch to the horizon, the sound of the waves hitting the beach gently, soothing them in the background.

Cecilia had outdone herself in putting the meal together for all of them, and Henry had brought the most delicious organic gluten-free sourdough bread along with Miyokos vegan butter. There was also the family-size organic salad they had made together with the veggies Veronica brought, along with Meghan's homemade apple cider vinegar, honey mustard dressing. Eric and Edward had put together an organic fruit platter for dessert with organic dark chocolate and Veronica had PowerShake samples to share with everyone, too.

Veronica didn't cook much at home because it was only her most of the time. When she and Margot had "meals" together—it had always been pizza or sushi or something to-go. Lately, Veronica had only been craving the Purium PowerShakes, and she had recently added steamed veggies with hummus, and fruit for dessert. It felt so nourishing on every level to share a meal and have it be organic whole foods. Veronica could imagine living her whole life like this, gathering with her Angelic family for meals that they created together at one another's homes, each with their Holy Beloved, encouraging one another on the path of life on Earth—a path that was filled with many complexities and much joy.

Veronica considered Eric's question about what to do next with Markus, pausing before responding as she absorbed all the beautiful imagery and wonder around her (while also savoring the pasta-salad bite she had just taken). "You know, typically I would wait. I would wait for him to reach out to me. I would wait for him to make a move, but that doesn't feel right in this situation. I could easily have messaged him while I was waiting at Salt when we had agreed to meet. But I got so taken out by the negative programming, I went into straight victim mode. I got totally lost in my wound of not being chosen and nothing working out for me. That's not my truth anymore. My truth is, I know that Markus and I have a special, sacred connection. I know he has free will to do whatever he wants to with that connection, but for me personally, I want to know that I did everything possible for us to come together in this life."

"That's my girl," Henry said with pride. "Breaking out of the cultural rules about how each individual should act in relationship is a massive liberation. Honoring each moment, each individual, each situation and letting your intuition guide you is the highest, most honorable way to relate with others. I'm seriously so proud of you, Veronica. That psychic pollution you received from the negative agenda could have easily taken you out for weeks or months even."

"Or years," Meghan added. "I've seen women and men let the whispers in their minds take them off the path for years, decades even, before they wake back up, reclaim their true Divine Power, and live in The Way they actually came to."

Henry agreed, "Exactly right, Meghan."

"So do Angelics, once they awaken to who they really are, have a responsibility to create different kinds of relationships to help the humans remember, too?" Veronica asked.

"Yes, they do," Edward said. "As an Angelic, we cannot fall prey to the machinations of the agenda, which creates and treats relationships like a prison. We have to model sacred relating, and honor when our sacred agreements are in effect, and when they close. It's such a disservice to a Soul when they stay too long in a relationship that has expired, and the same when they get caught up in power dynamics and do not enter Sacred Union when it's presented to them."

Veronica gently rubbed the center of her chest as the warming sensation expanded throughout her heart when Edward spoke. The Way of relating that Henry, Meghan, and

Edward shared was lighting something up within her. She felt liberated to know she was free of the rules set by society of boyfriend/girlfriend, husband/wife, lover/mistress. And that instead she could step into Sacred Union–honoring each relationship as a spiritual agreement, knowing it would last as long as it needed to.

"So wait, is it possible Cecilia and Edward that your spiritual agreement could come to completion?" Veronica asked, tearing off a piece of sourdough bread to nibble on.

They both started laughing. "Yes, of course," Cecilia said. "We have free will and our union can take on whatever configuration we both choose. We could decide to walk away at any time. But I think what you're asking, dear Veronica, is if there's an expiration date to a Holy Beloved or Divine Counterpart union. Is that right?"

Veronica nodded, and Edward continued, "Your Divine Counterpart is your eternal love. They are the one you return to throughout all of your lifetimes as well as in the non-physical realms. Of course, there are other loves throughout a life because there's one that exists for every dimension of consciousness. This helps humans and Angelics when they're in human form, grow and mature their capacity for love and sacred relationship."

Veronica's eyes must have bugged out of her head because Edward put his hand up and said, "Now don't worry, this isn't as complicated as you might think."

Cecilia jumped in, "Think of it like this Veronica. The majority of humans live in one or two dimensions of consciousness in each lifetime. So for them, they may have one to two true Loves of their Life. That's why most first marriages at least don't continue and shouldn't–humans are evolving faster now and they have more than one Love of their Life in any given lifetime. For us as Angelics, we have one Divine Counterpart, which is our highest-level love–think Mary Magdalene and Jesus or King Solomon and Queen Sheba. We can have other loves throughout our lifetime and we will until we're at the frequency of alignment with our Divine Counterpart, the other half of our Soul and Spirit, or highest dimensional love."

Veronica was starting to feel overwhelmed but also like she was on the verge of truly innerstanding what they were sharing.

"Could a human have a Divine Counterpart, the other half of their Soul?" she asked.

"No," everyone answered at once, breaking into laughter.

Meghan joined in, turning her eyes to Eric as she spoke. "Humans have a love of their life for every dimension of consciousness that they're vibrating in, or existing in exactly like Cecilia explained. It's only Angelics that incarnate with the other half of their Soul and who can choose to reunite with them."

"Oh wow," Veronica said, wondering if she should be taking notes as they shared all these important details with her.

"Don't take our word for it though Veronica, ask to be shown, and you will," Henry said, as he passed the salad to Cecilia, who was diving in for seconds.

"Ask to be shown?" she asked.

"Yes, pray at night or in meditation that you be shown what's truly true regarding all that's been shared with you tonight. That's how each of us knows all of this. We asked and were shown that this is how it works. Some were shown in images in their mind's eye, some heard an Angelic voice tell them this, some saw Source HerSelf come before them and share this Wisdom, and still others simply knew that this was the way sacred relating worked on Earth. So your Higher Self and spiritual team will make it known to you. That way you don't have to choose to believe what we're telling you or not, you can *know* it for yourself."

"Okay, whoa. I will do that. Thank you, Henry. But before I do, I want to go back to Edward and Cecilia. You know you're Holy Beloved Divine Counterparts, you've chosen to be in a romantic relationship on Earth, I see you each wearing rings which are a symbol in the matrix of marriage. How does that work? And if you wanted, even as Divine Counterparts, could you choose to no longer be unified romantically?" Veronica felt determined to ground in more of the details of how relationship worked for Angelics *and* for humans–especially if she was going to be helping them as an Angelic at some point in the future. She wiped her hands on her indigo blue linen napkin and leaned in, eager to learn more.

"I love how your mind works, Veronica," Cecilia said, as she took a sip of kombucha. "Yes, as I mentioned, even though Edward and I know we're Angelics, and we know we're Divine Counterparts, if we get disconnected from Source and our path together, we *could* choose to end our romantic union on Earth. But Edward and I do not have any plans to do so. Our intention now is to shine the Light of what Sacred Union looks like on Earth and bring that Light everywhere we go. We've just expanded to teach workshops for couples. This will be another way our expanded Angelic family can find us, and also for us to support humans in their relationships."

Meghan clapped as Cecilia shared this last bit of news, clearly excited about this new expansion in Edward and Cecilia's work on Earth.

"And to answer your other question," Edward said, as he buttered a piece of bread. "Divine Counterparts do not have to get married, as they are already unified in the Angelic Realms. *And* if they want to play married in the artificial matrix's legal marriage construct while on Earth, they most certainly can. We chose to have a spiritual ceremony honoring our union, and we exchanged rings as part of that because long before it was part of the mainstream agenda, it was something the ancient Egyptians did when they came into union with their Beloved. Why? The ring finger on the left hand is directly connected to the heart, and so exchanging rings and wearing them energetically is a symbol of unifying two hearts together as one."

"Wow. This keeps getting more and more interesting. Can I see your rings?" Veronica said.

Cecilia, sitting across the table from her, placed her hand in front of Veronica, showcasing a rose-gold Celtic knot, with an emerald in the center.

"Beautiful," Veronica murmured.

Edward, sitting next to his Holy Beloved Cecilia, showed Veronica his ring as well, a rose-gold band made up of Celtic knots.

"Thank you. I'm loving this so much. I wish this was something I had learned about in school," said Veronica playfully. "It would have made my relationship life a lot easier."

Meghan and Eric agreed enthusiastically, "That's Eric's and I dream. We're starting small with it, but one day we would like to have a school for children to teach them these real-life principles. Right now Eric has a small preschool that I help with when I'm not at the bookstore. We're setting the intention that this grows into a larger creation over time. Maybe even someday having Edward and Cecilia teach sacred relating to older students."

Veronica was awestruck. She loved learning about how each Holy Beloved couple was supporting the expansion of the collective consciousness.

Each face beamed at her. She could feel their exuberance for her, for this path, and for all that they were each uncovering during their life on Earth.

"We've all been where you are Veronica, these initial stages of awakening to who you really are is magical and a time of learning and remembering. We're honored to assist you as you do," Cecilia said.

"And girl, you're only getting started–it gets better and better from here," Eric said, putting his arm around Meghan.

Veronica lit up. "I can't wait! And I still have a million more questions, but I'll save them for another time while I digest all that you've shared with me tonight, along with this delicious meal!"

Veronica wanted to hear more about Meghan and Eric's union, and she wanted to know what was up with Henry. She knew he had dated several beautiful and brilliant women from what Meghan had told her briefly at work. She couldn't wait to hear everyone's story, but for now, she had to sort out her own unfolding. Markus had either completely ghosted her or something had happened that had interfered with him showing up, maybe something like what she had experienced with the negative thoughtforms appearing and telling him lies about what he deserved. She owed herself and him the opportunity to get clear about what was going on between them.

I've been playing the victim my whole life. Without even realizing it. I've been waiting for the bookstore to show up for me to buy, waiting for the money to show up to buy the bookstore, waiting for my dream house and the money for that, waiting for my partner, waiting for the world to realize who I really am. But I haven't honored and realized who I really was, so how could the world?!

Any time I did take action, if something went wrong, I would crumple into a pile on the floor convinced it meant it wasn't for me and I couldn't have what I truly desired. I gave up on Soulmates in my teen years for Goddess sake! And I've hung on to the dream of owning my own bookstore without doing more than working at a bunch of different shops, hoping someone would gift me the money and opportunity. It's ludicrous!

With these startling realizations, Veronica wondered how many other humans and Angelics were living in this same way, sabotaging their deepest fulfillment and happiness. Never claiming their Divine heritage, prosperity, and love. Veronica shook her head as she drove home from the gathering, thinking of all the needless broken hearts and tragic storylines circulating Earth.

If only they would remember...

CHAPTER 8

Right now, however, it was Veronica who needed to remember. She kept mulling over and over the conversation at dinner the night before with her Angelics family as she made the drive to the bookstore along the Oregon Coast Highway. There was an enormous amount for her to learn and grow into, and it excited her. Maybe enough to keep her from risking it all with Markus. She looked briefly out at the sea, and her gut clenched.

She could easily see herself getting so wrapped up in her spiritual studies of meditation, prayer, and gatherings with her Angelic family that she avoided asking Markus about what had happened with their date. Rejection was terrifying, especially if he was her Divine Counterpart. Because if he didn't want her, then what hope was left for her when it came to love? She had already faced so much disappointment and heartache first with her parents as a child and then with just about every romantic partner she had. Could she take a risk for a love this big?

Veronica continued to draw strength from the encouragement of Cecilia and Edward, and Henry too. She could do this, she told herself as she pulled into the small parking lot of Books on the Beach. She told herself she could even accept the rejection from Markus if that's what occurred. Because what she did know for sure was that she could not live without knowing, really knowing, what could be between them. And so Veronica did something she had never in her life done before in the realm of a romantic relationship. As she sat in her car outside the mystical bookstore where she had finally found her purpose after years of struggling, she took out her phone and prayed over it.

"Oh Holy One, God-Goddess, Source HerSelf be with me now as I know you always are. Bless my text to Markus Mullins. May the Highest Destined outcomes take place for our union. If we are truly Holy Beloved Divine Counterparts, may it be crystal clearly made known to us. May Markus feel my heart through this message and may I feel his. May the Highest Divine Will be done in service to all. And so it is. It is so."

With that, Veronica began typing her text to Markus. She was either delusional or stepping into a new level of her Angelic superpowers. "We shall see," she whispered silently to herself.

"Hey, Markus! I had it on the calendar for us to meet yesterday at 2 p.m. I went to Salt and was there until about a quarter to 3 p.m. and then left when I didn't see you there. Did I get our time wrong? Or did something come up? If so, would you like to reschedule? Wishing you a Light-filled day, XV 🤍"

Veronica could not believe she was going to send this text. But apparently, that's what happens when you pray over your communications. Never in her wildest dreams would she follow up on a guy ghosting her, let alone ask about rescheduling in the very same message. Perhaps she was setting herself up for a big fall, but something within her prodded her to do it, anyway. So she did. Veronica hit send, said, "Thank you, Great Spirit," got out of her car, and headed into work.

Henry was at the front of the store, shifting out the main display, as she entered. They made eye contact, smiling at each other, and in that smile and eye contact, Henry asked with his mind, "Did you reach out to Markus yet?"

And Veronica responded, "Yes, just sent the text!" To which Henry replied, "Well done, Angelic one," with a chuckle.

As Veronica strolled to the back of the shop to put her things in her cubby, she halted in her tracks. What in the heck? Had they? Henry had followed her, and she spun around to face him.

"Um, we just had a conversation...with our MINDS," she stuttered.

"Yes, you are correct. This is what daily meditation, organic superfoods, and gathering with your Angelic family will do," he said.

"Telepathic communication??" Veronica asked.

"Yep," Henry said. "And that was only a basic conversation. After you unite with your Holy Beloved Divine Counterpart and increase your innerstanding of life on Earth as an Angelic, your capacity will grow and develop even more. You and your Beloved will be able to have whole conversations telepathically, without interference, like what often happens with technological communications."

He walked out of the employee area to let Veronica chew on *that* revelation for a moment.

They were not kidding when they said it keeps getting better and better, but they could have also told me that it keeps getting weirder and weirder, too.

Later that day, as Veronica was restocking their sold-out new releases, Meghan popped in to get her schedule for the week. Henry asked if the three of them could talk for a moment, so they gathered at the tall oak checkout desk to chat.

"So, I've decided to bring in crystals from Brazil to the shop," Henry announced, tucking his hands in the pockets of his brown corduroy pants that he had paired with a turquoise and brown plaid button up shirt. "I know we've traditionally only carried rose quartz here, and that's because rose quartz is the official gemstone of the Angelics."

Veronica glanced over at the small case of rose quartz that they had by the Angels book section near the front of the shop. Pink stones, mostly rough and uncut in a variety of shades of pink glistened in the case. Finally she understood why they had been there all along.

Henry continued, "However, I was shown in a dream that I need to bring in some amethyst, clear quartz, shungite, and selenite to offer our customers. I was shown that it will be best if these gemstones come direct from mines in Brazil. I'll be purchasing our crystals from a friend I have in Brazil who can get them basically direct from the crystal mines. I also know that this mine uses a more holistic approach, by praying over the area and asking the Earth for permission before extracting the crystals. And that's very important to me because it means that energetically the crystals will have a higher vibrational countenance rather than trauma as they're honored from the beginning for their service on Earth."

Meghan's eyes lit up, as she set down her "Metaphysical AF" canvas tote bag, giving a better view of her long, colorful beaded necklaces. "I love this, Henry! You know I have a special connection to crystals, and even though this is a bookstore, I could feel that crystal healing would be of benefit to our customers."

"Yes, you know I wasn't going to be an Angelic with a crystal shop, but I *can be* an Angelic with a high-vibration bookstore featuring a few of the highest-vibrational crystals. I would love to have you oversee the crystals that come in, Meghan. And on the days you work, when customers are looking for crystals or are intrigued by our stock, you'll help find the right match for them."

"The right match? Meaning there are certain crystals for certain people?" Veronica interrupted, folding her arms across her chest, shifting her weight to get more comfortable.

"Yes," Henry said. "Crystals are living entities here on Earth to assist humans in their healing and awakening. That's why they're a natural part of the Earth. So there'll be certain crystal types for certain humans and particular crystals within that type that will vibrate in alignment for an individual."

"For instance," Meghan said. "Rose quartz is a natural crystal for you as an Angelic Veronica, and because you're open to unifying with your Holy Beloved. It holds the Angelic frequencies of unconditional sacred love, healing, and Divine Truth. But if you picked up any ole' rose quartz, it may not be of benefit to you because the supplier may have compromised energy, or someone with not amazing energy held it for a long time before you, or something of that nature. So Henry is asking me to tune in to which rose quartz, in my example, would be in harmony for you or for the customer I was helping. I do this by scanning my hand over the crystals and waiting until I feel a ping for the right crystal for that person."

"Why don't you do that now for Veronica, if you wouldn't mind, Meghan, to demonstrate it to her?" Henry asked. The shop was quiet, so it was the perfect time for Meghan to show one of her superpowers to Veronica.

"I'd love to," she said.

Veronica watched as Meghan placed her hands over the display with the rose quartz crystals in it, her eyes closed. Her hands began to move over the crystals in a graceful manner. Then, suddenly, a smile crossed her face, her eyes opened and she picked up an oddly shaped, raw rose quartz stone that was the lightest shade of pink Veronica had ever seen.

"Here," she said, offering the crystal to Veronica. "This one is yours. This one will help you with your Holy Beloved Divine Counterpart and in experiencing more unconditional love in your life."

Veronica cupped the stone in her hands and could instantly feel a vibration as she held it. "Do I need to do anything more with it?"

"Meditate with it daily, and you'll form an even closer bond with the stone and it will bless you with all things love," Meghan said.

～

When Veronica got home that evening, Margot was on a business call, negotiating a seller's listing price, so Veronica retreated to the kitchen. She couldn't wait to make herself some organic pasta and sauce, having been inspired by her dinner at Cecilia and Edward's.

After reading a ton of information on the Purium site and through various rabbit holes she had gone down online, she realized that after eating mostly fruit and PowerShakes for a month, she was ready to add in at least one hot meal a day for grounding nourishment. She learned from her online research that whatever she put into her body should be organic, as the U.S. food and beverage supply had been compromised by glyphosate toxicity from popular weed killers used for decades on agricultural crops and heavy metals, along with other environmental toxins. From her conversations with Henry and her Angelics family she learned that the pollution of the food and water supply blocked Angelics from receiving communication from their Divine Counterpart and, for humans, it served as a blockage to them coming together with the Love of their Life in whatever dimension of consciousness they were residing in. It also blocked both humans and Angelics from clear communication with their spiritual teams and Source as it polluted their bodies.

Over time, the body would exhibit signs of dis-ease through symptoms, as the body's functions became compromised and weighed down by the herbicides, heavy metals, and other environmental toxins. While the human body was created to regenerate and self-heal, the high use of poisons overtook the advanced technology of the body, which resulted in negative or painful body symptoms and dis-ease. These symptoms were the body's way of communicating with the Soul that it needed further detox.

Veronica had seen that the company Purium, which created her now beloved PowerShake, also offered 90-day cleanse and detox kits and she was considering doing that next. In the meantime, she had added cracked cell chlorella and ionic elements to her PowerShake to help her body continue releasing any toxins and heavy metals it had been exposed to from the food, beverage, and water supply. She now made sure that everything she picked up at the co-op was organic. She was committed to keeping her Angelic channel clear for the highest communication with her Divine Counterpart, spiritual team, and Source HerSelf.

A few minutes later, as she stirred her pasta sauce and the organic gluten-free pasta water boiled, she instinctively picked up her phone. Her text to Markus from earlier that morning said, "Failed to send." Veronica sighed, disappointed, and wondered if there was some artificial matrix interference with her and Markus's communication. Or if it was her own wounds and fears that were impeding their connection.

Whatever it was, she would not be deterred. She took a breath and visualized Markus and her embracing, recreating the sensations and frequency from her dreams with him. Then, she resent the message. Within a few minutes, her phone dinged again and Veronica grimaced. Why wasn't the text going through? Was she being blocked from messaging him? Much to her surprise, however, it was a reply from Markus.

"V, I'm so sorry we couldn't meet yesterday. I was getting ready to reach out to you to reschedule, so your timing is perfect. Embarrassingly, I had asked my biz mgr to put our date on my calendar & either she got the time wrong or I gave it to her incorrectly. I showed up at 3 p.m. yesterday, which just so happened to be when Salt closed. I can't believe I missed you by 15 minutes. 🙇 This isn't the first time something like this has happened. But that's a story for another time. All that to say, I'm happy you reached out. Let's reschedule. Want to try for this Friday, at noon at Salt? XM 🤍"

Veronica gulped, stopping what she was doing and placing her hand on her heart. Her risk had paid off. Their date *had* gotten interfered with by outside forces, which is something Cecilia and her Angelic family had warned could happen. And while she wasn't clear yet why he didn't message her from Salt, it did sound as though he had some negative agenda interference from his business manager and label. Whatever it was, it was enough to keep him from reaching out to her immediately. She was even more encouraged that he had called her V and signed off with an X and a heart, just as she had. Maybe he really was her Divine Counterpart!

Just cool your jets, V. You don't even know this guy yet.

Fortunately, Veronica had Friday off from the bookstore. This time though, she wasn't taking any chances, and she encouraged Markus to do the same.

"Maybe this sounds too weird, but it seems like we had some interference in meeting, so perhaps this time, we should both say a prayer of protection over our meet-up. Maybe we should ask that The Way be made clear & that we're able to connect with ease. What do you think? 🤍" she texted.

She cringed, unsure if Markus would think she was the strangest being ever. But, again, he surprised her.

"Yes something was interfering, for sure. I'm a big fan of prayer, so this works for me. I'll say a prayer for us to meet with ease this week. XOM 🤍"

This was perhaps too good to be true, but Veronica would not let any negative talk from her mind get in the way of her potential Sacred Union. She wrote back, "Perfect, see you at noon on Friday. XOV 🤍" and intended with power and enthusiasm for the highest outcome to take place.

≈

117

And take place, it did.

From the moment Markus walked into Salt and saw Veronica sitting on that sapphire blue couch, the two were instantly bonded.

"Psychic interference squashed," he said, scooping her up into a big hug.

It felt like they had gone to battle, albeit a small one, to even be standing in front of each other. Veronica felt a twinge of Light shoot through her heart and pelvis when he hugged her, and she wondered if he had felt the same thing. They stood there looking at one another in a bit of shock and wonder for a moment.

Veronica had attempted to be less obsessive about what to wear for this date and had quickly chosen a razorback rose pink tank (as a nod to her Angelic rose quartz), high-waisted skinny jeans, nude sandals, and a black cardigan sweater, worn sexily off one shoulder. Her eyes took in Markus and she loved what she saw. He was clearly trying to keep a low profile in a black baseball cap, simple black tee, and black jeans with black and white Nikes.

After a moment, Markus smiled and said in his sweet, gentle voice, "Want to order something?"

This snapped Veronica back into physical reality and pulled her out of the vortex that was the sparkle in Markus's radiant blue eyes.

"Oh yeah, that's what we're here for, right?"

Markus said, "Well, it's not the only reason we're here," as he touched her arm. "But it'll get us started."

They approached the counter in the back of the cafe. Veronica ordered a Pink Lady apple kombucha on tap (her favorite way to have kombucha) and a cup of their garden veggie soup with a slice of gluten-free bread. Whenever given the choice, Veronica chose gluten-free, as her stomach seemed to prefer it over wheat.

Markus turned to her, resting his hand on the small of her

back after she ordered. "I like the way you eat, lady." He turned back to the cashier and ordered the same thing she had.

God, why is he so adorable?

He leaned in again to her. "Just so you know, that was going to be my order before I heard yours."

"Sure, likely story," Veronica teased.

"Are you Markus Mullins?" the cashier asked.

"I am, but try not to tell anyone, okay?" Markus said, pulling his baseball cap down low over his eyes a bit more. "We're trying to have a quiet lunch, so I want to have some privacy."

"Yes, of course. I would recommend maybe you two eat at one of those tables back there–that way you'll be more tucked away and folks won't see you. I'll bring you your order instead of calling your name too. That way it won't draw more attention to you being here."

"That's perfect. Thank you, Kailey. That's your name, right?"

Kailey agreed enthusiastically; her name tag proudly displayed on her black Salt shirt.

"Thank you for your kindness," Markus said. "We appreciate it."

Veronica couldn't help but catch the word "we" and feel a flutter of butterflies in her stomach.

Markus turned to her, pointing to a few of the small table and chair sets located near the very back right side of Salt, "Are you okay with sitting at the table over here so we're more out of the way?"

"Of course, let's do it," she said.

Once they sat down, Kailey immediately brought over their kombuchas. "Thank you," they said together which made them both smile.

Veronica leaned in. "So is this like a thing for you, being famous and having to secure your privacy all the time?"

Markus sighed. "You know, here on the Coast, cuz it's my

hometown, and we're a hometown band, people are surprisingly cool. Locals don't bother me much. They'll maybe wave or say 'hi', but other than that, they really do honor my privacy. It's the folks from the city. If they're here at the Coast, they'll want a selfie, an autograph, that kind of thing. Honestly, I struggle with it.

"My whole life I wanted to make it big with my music. I wanted to be recognized for it. I wanted a hit record, and I visualized being on The Tonight Show. Hell, I even prayed that this would happen. And I'm super grateful for it, don't get me wrong. I've loved every minute. But after a decade of it, I just, I don't know. I'm craving something different, although I don't know exactly what. Maybe something more private, you know?" Markus paused in thought, taking a drink of his kombucha before he continued.

"Our hometown show that you were at, that's gonna be our last home show, and I've got a couple more in Portland and Eugene, but then that's it for a while. At least, that's what I'm thinking now. I want a break from it all. The two other guys, Stewy and Chad, they have some other music projects they want to work on too, although they would be devastated if I shut down the band entirely. They've made a lot of money from my songs over the years, we all have.

"Not to mention, there's a lot of interference from my label that I'm noticing with what I'm writing, who I spend time with, and my schedule–like you and I've already experienced. I'm a grown-ass man. I don't know if I can continue to live my life being micromanaged like that. I want to play with the possibility of what the next evolution of my music looks like. How I can create it, and get the frequency and energy of my message out in a way that's less traditional and less controlled. But, if I'm honest, with myself and with you, it *is* scary. Am I really ready to let it all go, especially since it's everything I've ever wanted and have worked for. You know?"

Veronica could feel the struggle Markus was in and she

could relate. Doing what the heart and Soul felt was the right path or caving to the pressure of those who wanted you to be like them was sincerely difficult. She felt incredible love and compassion for him and nodded to let him know she was right there with him.

"You know, the music industry must evolve too at some point. Incessant touring and being a slave to record companies and the media—that has to stop for everyone, and I think I'm at that juncture for myself of reevaluating it all. So I guess that's a long-winded answer to your question, but that's the truth. I'm hunkering down a bit at my house here on the Coast after the last few tour stops, and praying for clarity about a new way forward. A way that isn't tied up in the corporatized control game, which honestly is pretty wicked, but I'll spare you all the gory details, for now."

Veronica observed him as he spoke. She saw heavy murkiness around him when he spoke of the music industry and its control mechanisms. And she saw a beautiful, radiant Light come in as he talked about finding his own way, a way truer to who he truly was to share his frequency and messages. She couldn't even believe he had used the word frequency. He was far deeper than she could have imagined.

"What, what are you thinking? That I'm crazy? Ungrateful?" Markus interrupted her thoughts.

"Oh no, quite the opposite. I was watching your energy while you spoke. So much Light came into your eyes and around you when you talked about doing music in your own way and leaving behind some of those old, wicked structures. This might seem odd to say, but I'm proud of you. It takes a lot of courage to live the American fame dream and then realize that it's more entrapment than anything else."

Markus agreed and his body visibly relaxed. "Wow, you really get it. You don't think I sound ungrateful?"

"No, not at all. We can be grateful for someone or something and have the wisdom to know when our time with it is complete." Veronica wasn't entirely sure what had come over her. It was like being in his presence called forth a wiser version of herself.

"And I don't mean to act like I'm a victim of the music industry either. I've fully participated; I was even happy to do so. I was happy to sign over a lot of my privacy and rights and turn my power over to these men. That's what 'making it' is. But now, the next evolution of what it looks like for *me* to be a musician wants to be born. I think I might be a leader in this, so I have to pave a new way, you know? I have moments where I feel so sure and so clear about this, but frankly I wobble. I worked hard to get here, and I'm torn about letting it go, especially with so much at stake."

"I can so feel that for you, Markus. It's exciting when you talk about charting a new path though. And think of what it will inspire in other musicians who no doubt feel the same as you do."

Kailey brought over their soup and bread, not interfering with their conversation, simply setting it down in front of them and nodding as they thanked her.

"They're so sweet here," Veronica said.

"Yeah, I know the owner and they've always been cool with me coming here and making sure I don't get too much attention when I do, even when they have new staff I've never met before, like Kailey. That's why I was so excited when you said it was your favorite place. It was perfect because that meant I wouldn't have to explain the need to go to a private place to meet, and all that comes with spending time with me." He smiled genuinely over at her.

Veronica met him with her own bright and shining grin. Their eyes took one another in, an energy stirring between them, an energy that was new to them both.

"Hey, when we're finished here, would you want to come over to my studio? I would love to share with you some new songs I'm working on right now."

Go to his studio? The studio where the songs that were opening her heart were made? Veronica took a long breath to try to calm herself.

"Or, if that's too much, I totally understand too," Markus interjected.

Veronica couldn't believe he had the same kinds of insecurities as she had. This only made her relax more into the space with him and trust him even more.

"No, I would love to go. I was just thinking about how amazing it would be to be in the space where you create your music. It's like your ashram."

"No way, you did not say that."

"Say what?" Veronica asked.

"Ashram. That's exactly what I tell my band and close friends, that the studio is like my ashram. It doesn't translate with my band or label because, as it turns out, they're atheists and I'm the only one who believes in God and the miracles that come from that spiritual relationship. They think I'm a bit loopy, but it's my songs that have made us all famous and wealthy, so they play along."

"You're surrounded by atheists and you believe in spirituality and miracles? She pressed a hand to her heart in surprise. Then, she asked, "Why do you think you did that to yourself?"

"It's a good question. At first, I thought maybe it was so I could show them through my life and what I was able to create with our music that there's a Higher Power that loves us that we can tap into that will guide The Way. But now, with my band, the record label–I mean they're obviously not aligned with the magic of life, unless, of course, it's gonna make them billions of dollars–so now I'm starting to wonder if I went on this whole fame ride so that I could return to my true self. Maybe so I could return to my true calling, to bring healing through my music and to show that someone can break free of the corporatized music industry control systems and pave their own way." Markus shrugged, running a hand through his brown curls. "But who knows? Like I said, I've been praying about it to find clarity."

"Are you thinking of leaving the band and going out on your own, then?"

"Um, yeah. Yeah, I am. I want a richer life, the kind of richer you can't get when you have mainstream fame and success. You know?" Markus looked into Veronica's eyes and as he did, she saw light flecks of gold emanate briefly from his irises.

It was a ways to his studio, and Markus offered to drive Veronica in his red Tesla. She agreed, noting that typically she would never do something like this on a first date with anyone. She preferred to drive her own car to make sure she always had an exit strategy if she needed it. But this was Markus Mullins. And she was about to be alone with him, in his studio, where he wrote and created hit songs.

Even better, they seemed to have an authentic connection. *Unless he's simply trying to get into your pants,* she heard the voice of her best friend Eloise pop in. *What?! No, El, your opinion is not allowed here,* she telepathically said back and focused on the road ahead.

Markus handed Veronica a steaming cup of organic dandelion root tea with organic almond milk and raw, Oregon honey as she sat on the comfy, beat-up orange and yellow plaid couch in his studio; his guitar, keyboards, and audio recording equipment behind him.

"I stopped drinking alcohol a few years ago," he said, sitting down next to her. "It's not good for the body, my voice, my health, or good decision-making I found. I had a bad experience–getting too drunk, a bunch of groupies, you get the idea. After that, I swore off booze, and since that day, I've made a lot better decisions."

"You've got to be one of the only musicians smart enough to do that without an intervention or head-lining humiliation. You should teach a workshop about giving up alcohol and how it allows your creativity to expand," Veronica suggested, taking a sip of the sweet and earthy tea.

"Yeah, well it's just me and a bunch of former alcoholic musicians that quit, it seems. I'm not sure how many would sign up for a workshop about that. Alcohol is positioned as a socially acceptable form of poison and it's clearly used to control the masses and keep individuals from living their destinies. I also realized from the experience I mentioned that it's called spirits for a reason. Alcohol opens people up to a bunch of energies that can suck their life force, especially if someone is highly sensitive."

Veronica was taking it all in as he spoke, wondering if she was someone who would also be considered highly sensitive. "It's weird, when I had my spiritual awakening the week of your concert and then *at* your concert–ever since then I cannot bring myself to drink alcohol. All I want are these organic superfood smoothies, fruit, and super high-vibe foods."

"I went through something similar actually, maybe not the spiritual awakening part," Markus said, "although we'll have to discuss what qualifies as one, I suppose. I went through an intensive phase of only wanting superfoods, fruits, and smoothies. I now make sure I do a cleanse a couple of times a year to keep my health in check. You know, at minimum, for a greater quality of life. I hear friends say, 'Everyone dies, so who cares? Live it up now!' but for me, this life isn't one big hedonistic excursion anymore.

"I already lived that way and I felt horrible in my body. I know somehow intuitively that how I treat my body and my life now affects where I go after this life. I also know that when I eat processed foods, I feel terrible. My creativity is nothing compared to what it is when I'm cleansing or eating in a way that's organic and nourishing to my body. For me, it was realizing that it took half the time it normally did for me to write an album when I was fasting and cleansing than it did when I was eating the conventional American diet. One of my mom's friends has a website that has what she calls high-vibrational recipes and recommendations, if you ever want to check it out."

Veronica was stunned by his eloquence, his maturity, and his ability to think for himself. That alone was often non-existent on Earth. She couldn't throw a stick and not hit a whole gaggle of humans who were merely following the program of what everyone else was doing. As she mulled over what he had shared, she settled into the couch, placing one of the light-yellow décor pillows behind her back, and setting her tea mug on the coffee table in front of them.

"Wow, I feel so much less alone knowing I'm not the only one who has gone through something like this with the food piece," she said. "And yeah, I would love it if you could text me the website. I'll check it out. I've fallen deeply in love with this Purium PowerShake. Have you tried it? And I think they have a cleanse too that I've been feeling like checking out."

Markus responded enthusiastically, "Yes, those are the superfoods I take and the cleanses I do! You should try the 90-day ULT health reset, especially when you're just getting started. I do it every year or so, and it's upleveled my creativity, intuition, and overall physical health. Especially when I was touring intensely and barely getting any sleep, because we were in a different city every night. I don't get sick anymore, and when I do, it's like one- or two-days max and then I'm back to feeling good."

Veronica beamed at him. It was so surprising all the things they had in common. She heard her heart whisper that it wasn't *actually surprising* if he was her Divine Counterpart and an

Angelic. It was normal for them to have so much alignment. Although she wasn't sure when she would bridge that subject with him just yet. How does one say, "Hey I'm an Angel, do you think you might be one too?"

She'd have to go there some other time. For now, she wanted to take what he shared earlier and expand on it more. "You mentioned that you know that how you treat your body and your life now sets you up or makes a difference for wherever you go to next after you leave your body. I love that perspective and I'm uncovering so much about the spiritual path at this point in my life. I would love to know about your experience, however much you feel called to share, that is."

Markus was tuning his guitar as they talked, and paused, soaking up her question. "Sure, of course. I was raised very religious, and as I grew up, I was able to let go of the man-made aspects and connect more to God through nature. The one thing I hung onto from my time in religion was prayer. It's become an important part of my life. I honestly had to do it as my 'fame' grew--" Markus used quotes with his hands around the word fame. "I had to pray to stay grounded in myself. It's easy to get swept up in the hype, especially when the hype is about you.

"So I quit drinking alcohol as we hit our peak, started eating organic and incorporating the Purium superfoods into my daily life, and made prayer a part of my daily lifestyle too. It helped quiet the noise of the media, shows and fans, and all that comes with the touring life. During these times of prayer, I've had the feeling, the sense that what I'm doing now in this life is not only about now. It's creating a frequency that extends further into the future and is literally calling to me my next experience in this life and in the life to come. I don't know how I know there are more lives than this one. It's simply a knowing that has come to me from my daily practices. You know, I rarely talk about this, though, because most of the people around me wouldn't be able to connect to this kind of conversation. My other two bandmates think I'm silly with all my practices."

Veronica's heart and Soul were filling to the brim with massive levels of love and adoration for Markus as she listened to him. She placed her hand on his and he smiled.

"Thank you for sharing this with me, Markus. It means so much to my heart to hear about your experience, it encourages and inspires me. And I also want to thank you for being in this world and showing up as a musician in this way. I know that how you're showing up *is* helping to seed a new archetype of what it means to be a successful singer/songwriter/musician here on Earth."

As Veronica spoke these words, her eye contact with Markus deepened and it felt as though there was a golden glow of light surrounding their bodies. Markus's eyes filled with tears and he nodded as she spoke, feeling the intensity and the alignment of what she shared. He *was* seeding a new vision of what was possible for those with musical gifts through how he showed up now, just as Veronica was seeding a new vision of how women could show up in front of their Holy Beloved. Open, wise, vulnerable, and free.

There was only silence now between them as they let themselves marinate in the moment of showing their true selves to each other. And then Markus spoke, in his quiet way.

"I do have a song I'd love to share with you. Are you open to me playing it for you?"

Is my life a freakin rom-com right now? YESSSS, I want you to play a guitar and sing to me, YES, Veronica's internal dialogue responded immediately.

Out loud she said, "Oh, Markus, that would be lovely."

The whole energy in the studio changed as Markus got up and grabbed a different guitar, setting down the one he'd been playing against the piano. She expected him to sit in front of her and share his song, but he didn't. He sat right next to her on the couch, turning his body to hers. Then, he began to play and sing the most beautiful song.

"I came to you in sunlight
I came to you in truth
Just to see the way your eyes Light up
Just to see the ways we could be together as One."

He truly was gifted. As he played, it seemed as if everything in the atmosphere stood at attention–all for him. Every molecule of aliveness that existed in that space now existed for him, including Veronica. Her body swayed to the music, her eyes closed, absorbing every word he uttered, every word he spoke.

After he finished playing, he stopped and peered intently into her eyes. Veronica clapped and gave him a small standing ovation.

"You are soooo gifted, it's mind-blowing," she said. And she meant it.

He grinned sweetly back at her.

"Thank you," he said. And he meant it.

Then, after taking a long pause, he said, "Let's talk about us. Is that okay with you?"

Veronica smiled, and he set his guitar down, moving closer to her on the couch.

"It's undeniable that there's a deep, I would say almost etheric, otherworldly connection, between us," he said.

A chill shot through her body and she bit her lip, nodding in agreement.

"I'm surprised by it and also not surprised. That we would meet at my hometown show, that we would have so much in common and so many synchronicities–it's magical, and it has fully captured my attention."

"Mine too," Veronica said softly.

"You've fully captured my attention, Veronica." Markus reached up and tucked one of her curls behind her right ear.

Veronica's eyes closed as she allowed herself to be

completely present to the softness of his touch, a flutter in her lower belly as his finger gently caressed the back of her ear.

"It seems as though we share a lot of mystical, spiritual interests, too. I don't exactly know what it is, but we're being united by something larger than ourselves. That much I can feel is true."

Veronica swallowed hard and nodded again. Was this really happening?! He was feeling it all too. She felt like she was living in one of the wildest dreams that she had ever had with him.

Then, the energy shifted and Markus disconnected their eye contact, moving his gaze, squinting as if trying to read his lines from across the room.

"Because this connection is so sacred, and so big, which denotes its importance in the stream of both of our lives, I don't want to pollute it in any way. It's almost like I need to handle our connection like it's a precious gemstone. I know I can't dive into a relationship with you or start dating you or being intimate with you. This is too special, and even though I do desire a relationship in the near future, being with me can be challenging because of all the outside factors that affect my life. While I'm toying with the idea of cutting myself loose from the larger system I'm a part of, I'm not free yet, and that makes this complicated."

Veronica felt a pang in her heart, realizing that this connection was so powerful that it was scaring him and causing him to push her away. For a moment she panicked internally, feeling as though she needed to gasp for breath. What could she say, what could she do to make him see? What could she do so that he would know who she was?

Without thinking she blurted out, "Markus, I agree with what you've said about the sacredness and bigness of our connection. I've felt that since, well, since the dreams I started having about you, and then when I remembered you from other lifetimes." She caught herself by surprise letting these words out, but she couldn't walk away from their conversation without him knowing that their connection was even bigger than he imagined. She held her breath and paused to gauge his reaction.

He raised his eyebrows. "You've remembered some of our lifetimes together? You've had dreams about...us?"

She let the air she had been holding in her lungs out and placed her palm on the center of her chest. "I have. Right before my sister got the tickets to your show, I started having a series of dreams with a man whose face I could not recognize, but they were the most delicious dreams I've ever had. I would wake up and want to go back to sleep to spend more time with him. The day before your hometown concert, I was finally shown the man's face. It looked familiar but I couldn't place it. It was only when my sister dragged me to the front of the stage that night and your head was tilted back in the same way as in my dream that I realized that it was you! It shook me."

Veronica knew she was taking a huge risk. While Markus was spiritual in his own way, the kind of experiences she'd been having could easily be seen as nutty. Would Markus accept her and her burgeoning gifts? Would he judge her or worse mock her? She took another breath, knowing she had no choice but to continue.

"When I got up close to the stage, I started seeing images flashing through my mind of us, living together in another time, having a family, all these things that I had never seen or contemplated before. I instantly burst into tears, and I could not control any of it. On top of that, all this energy was swirling in my heart and this feeling of the most Immense Love—it took my breath away. And I didn't even know you or anything about you. Then, after that, do you remember what you said to me when we met in that theater lobby?"

Markus seemed as shocked as she had been. He rubbed his arms and said, "V, whoa. I've got chills. This is so crazy. You've never had anything like this happen before?"

It was a good sign that this was his response and he wasn't

running for the door, she thought. "Never. And I know that it's a lot. It overwhelmed me, especially at first. For several days after, everywhere I went there was the name Markus, and people coming into the store looking for books by authors named Markus, your songs were at the grocery store and in the shop where I work and a woman was hollering after her son and his name was Markus. It was like the whole Universe was conspiring for us to come together. That's when I finally caved and messaged you on IG. I know this is intense and all of the things, and I'm not at all interested in convincing you of anything. But I'm also wondering, do you remember me? Do I seem familiar to you?"

"Oh, that's it, isn't it? I said, 'Don't I know you from somewhere?' I did, I remember that now. You felt familiar the moment I saw you. There was this shift in the energy, in the molecular structure around you, around us. There's a familiarity between us, but not from this time or this place." Markus closed his eyes, placing one of his hands on his heart.

Veronica sat there, breathing beside him, syncing her breath to his. He reached for her hand and held it in his for a beat. Then his eyes opened and looked into hers.

"Veronica, I don't fully know what's going on here. There's so much magic and synchronicity in our connection and, at the same time, I'm terrified by it. I'm so grateful for your vulnerability in sharing all of this with me, and I'm not going to lie, *it is* a lot. This is so precious and I cannot screw this up. And you've got to know, I usually screw things up." Markus chuckled in self-deprecation.

"I hear you Markus, I do, trust me. My last relationship ended nine months ago and it was tough. He realized he was in love with his best girl friend who we used to hang out with all the time."

"Oh, I'm sorry, V," Markus said, sounding genuinely apologetic.

She loved that he was calling her V, pulling that from her

texts. Simply hearing the sound of his voice saying her name or calling her V made her body tingle all over.

"Thank you, but that's not necessary. All that pain and drama led me here to this experience with you that has most definitely been the most magical connection I've ever had. I would like to see what would happen if we spent more time together, meditated together, and prayed together to see what could be. You know?"

Markus nodded, not making eye contact with her. He lifted Veronica's other free hand into his. She could feel the pulsing of their energies now. She could feel their hearts beating in unison, beating for each other. She could feel his fear, his withholding. She could feel a shadowy presence with him that did not want them together.

Veronica unleashed a big, jagged breath. She knew what this meant. He regarded her with tears in his eyes. He said nothing out loud in response, but Veronica could hear his words all the same. Already, their telepathic communication was strong.

"Maybe some other time, or lifetime, or maybe when the fear isn't gripping me like it is now. Maybe when the distorted entities lets go of me, maybe then we can be together. But it can't be now." He communicated it all to her through their hands entwined together as one.

Veronica wanted to cry, but she held back.

They both stood up and hugged. Except this was not a normal hug. As their bodies pressed together, an electricity filled with what Veronica could only describe as liquid love flooding her body. It was as if bringing their bodies together, fully clothed in an embrace, was a tease to their forms. Their bodies wanted to be closer, closer than an embrace, closer than anything the physical form could experience. Markus kept embracing her more, pressing his pulsing body into hers. Veronica could not help herself and she did the same, letting herself feel the sheer power of the Love and electricity that was coursing through them both. Their cheeks were against each other, breathing heavily, in unison.

"I didn't know they made hugs like this, Markus," Veronica whispered.

He laughed softly. "I didn't either V," he said.

Their noses touched; their eyes were closed, their breath continued to synch. They were caressing one another's faces so tenderly. It was so sexy, so magnificent Veronica could cry from the infinite sensations of Love and pleasure that were pouring forth from her body, from her Soul.

Markus cupped his hand to her face, holding it, placing his lips right in front of hers, just mere inches away. How she longed to merge with him, how her body was aching for him. He breathed into her, his lips there, now touching hers. His mouth parted, as did Veronica's, and he brought his fingers to her face, now giving her his tongue, and she took him in ecstatically, entwining her tongue with his. Nestled together in his music studio on the Oregon Coast, Veronica Walter and Markus Mullins began to remember one another again.

After several minutes of the most intentional and passionate kissing of her life, Markus took Veronica by the hand and led her further into the studio space, never breaking eye contact with her as he walked backward through the studio.

"Where are we going?" Veronica half whispered; half giggled. One part of her was ready to jump into bed with him. The other part knew that until they were both clear on their relationship with one another that sex would be a huge mistake for her heart.

"Somewhere we can be more comfortable," he mumbled.

He took them into a room within the studio that had, not to Veronica's total surprise, a queen-sized bed, complete with a sky-blue comforter and white and blue striped pillows.

Veronica had a moment of fear; did he think she was going to have sex with him right then? After he had implied that he was too afraid by the vastness of their connection? And after she had seen the murky energy gripping his Soul that wasn't allowing him to be with her?

Thankfully, that wasn't Markus's style; he was true to his word of desiring to honor the depth of their connection.

"I would love to lay here and hold you. Is that okay?" he asked.

This.Man.Is.A.Dream.

"Yeah, that sounds perfect," she said.

Markus lay on the bed, opening his arms for her to rest on his chest. They laid there like that for several minutes when Markus said, "That kiss though. What was happening there?"

Veronica looked up at him. "Right? Seriously, I had no idea that hugging and kissing could feel like that."

He smiled at her, shaking his head. "Oh Veronica, what am I going to do with you?" he mused as he squeezed her, moving his body into hers.

"Hmm...I could think of a couple of things for you to do with me. You know, after you let that huge cask of shadowy energy that's clinging to your field go," she said as truthfully and as lightly as she could.

Markus started cracking up. "A huge cask of shadowy energy, eh? Is that what you're picking up in my energy field now? Are you psychic now, sweet V?"

Veronica had never thought of herself as psychic but she had to admit, it was seeming that way. She felt so at ease in his presence that she could be her wise, Angelic self with him, an aspect of herself she had not ever been fully in touch with. "Only with you apparently, Markus. When we were at Salt talking and then tonight when we were holding hands and breathing together, and you shared you were afraid, I saw it." She met his gaze, and his expression was serious as he considered her words.

Veronica didn't intend to make him uncomfortable, so she shifted to a lighter topic, "But we don't have to talk about what that is or why it's there if you're not ready, cuz I have another Markus mystery I would like to solve. I'm super curious–in the most benign way of course, why is there a bed in your music studio?"

He laughed again, this time loudly in a way that shook both of their bodies. Veronica adjusted her body to be more centered over his, studying him to get the full answer.

"I suppose it seems a bit salacious, doesn't it? The truth is I often work late into the night, by myself or with the guys, and I'll crash here so I don't have to drive all the way home. I was grateful to be gifted this studio by one of my patrons many years ago when I was first getting started with my music career. I was pretty much broke, waiting tables and I lived here for a few years before things took off."

"Well, that now explains the shower in the bathroom too, so thanks for clarifying," Veronica teased.

Markus squeezed her. She looked up at him, their lips only inches apart. He was too alluring to resist, so she shifted her weight, placing her lips upon his.

Veronica woke up in the early morning hours, cold ... and alone. She sat up in the bed she had shared with Markus, a soft glow emanating from the other room. Still in her clothes from the night before, she walked into the studio space to find Markus sitting there with a cup of tea, his guitar, and a notebook.

"Hey, I hope I didn't wake you. Was I being too loud?" he asked.

"No, not at all. I can't believe we passed out for the night. I slept so hard, it was crazy."

Markus grinned at her. "I know, I slept great, too. You fell asleep with your head on my chest. It was really sweet. I woke up around 5 a.m. though with a song moving through me so I had to grab my notebook to get it down on paper."

"I love that. Sometimes I feel that way about books. I'll wake up early and be so excited to go unpack a new shipment or dive into the newest book that's come into the shop. When you love something fully, it seems to work like that . . ." Veronica said, her voice trailing off.

"Hey, come sit down here." Markus patted the couch next to him. As she did, he draped a soft orange cashmere blanket over her legs. He grabbed her hand. "Last night was beautiful. You are beautiful."

Veronica covered her face. "Thank you, and I'm not too sure I could imagine that being true first thing in the morning."

"Well, imagine it, because it's true." He kissed her hand as he said this. "I'm so happy that we've met, that life has brought us together in this way, and that we've had this time together. And I want to be transparent with you because our connection feels so big, and so sacred."

Veronica's stomach tightened. She knew what he was going to say before he even said it, and tears filled her eyes.

"Last night, I felt clear that I couldn't move forward with you. And then, that hug. And those kisses, and you know, spending the night together." Markus looked at her sheepishly. They had moved into full make-out mode that night although they hadn't gotten completely naked. Either way, it was evident to both of them that their sexual connection was strong and pulsing with life.

He continued, "Now, I'm confused. I don't want to fuck it up, and I don't want to hurt you. You're too special for that. I want you in my life in some capacity, no matter what we decide to do. My life, the touring, the music, the opportunities, that cask of murky energy you saw, which I'm pretty sure is the music industry that I'm a part of...While a part of me wishes to create something different like I shared with you yesterday, those pieces are still active in my life right now. And it's a lot, and it's a lot on relationships, and I wouldn't want to put you through that unnecessarily. You know what I mean?"

Veronica cleared her throat and shook her head to wake herself up a bit more. She couldn't believe that after their night together, after their conversations, after the otherworldly energy that was present with them that he would come to this conclusion. Why was this happening to her, her wounded self cried out internally.

"I hear what you're saying. I disagree with you, but only because I've been shown so clearly in my dream state and through our connection that this is something more than a traditional relationship. This is holy, and it *is* big and sacred like you say. And if you're not ready for that, then I have to respect it," Veronica said as she looked down, unable to fully process what was happening.

They were quiet for a moment, and then Markus said the worst thing of all. "Can I drive you back to your car?"

Once Veronica was in her car outside of Salt, she let the tears flow. And flow they did. This time not from being discarded by a man who didn't love her. This time they flowed because he *did* love her, and she loved him. She saw it in his eyes and felt it massively in her Soul. And that was not enough.

It wasn't enough to penetrate through his fears, it wasn't enough to blast through the negative agenda of the music industry that hung in his energy field like a heavy coat. It just wasn't enough. She couldn't believe it, and yet she could all at the same time. Veronica knew now with absolute certainty that she was an Angelic. What happened when one's Angelic Holy Beloved Divine Counterpart didn't want the other? She didn't know what was next, but for now, she was going to let herself cry.

As she drove home, she wondered what she would tell

Margot, Eloise, and her spiritual Angelic family...again. How could she explain the presence of them together and the energy that surged between them? How could she explain the power of their embrace and the erotic tenderness of their kisses? It wasn't like embracing or kissing anyone else. It had magic in it. It had Light in it. It had everything her heart and Soul had ever wanted.

What was so ironic was that even though her heart ached in a way Veronica had not known before; she also felt a new level of faith. She had intuitively known from the time she was small that this kind of love existed. And while she had abandoned that notion long ago after having her heart broken as a teenager, it had returned to her through a series of dreams. *The truth always returns*, she heard a small voice inside her say. It had been proven to her. The dreams were real, and their connection was real, but what they did with that connection, like Cecilia had said, was up to each of them and their free will choices.

As she drove home, she mentally calculated a list of horrible possibilities, barely noticing the way the big Douglas Fir trees swayed as gusts of wind came in from the ocean. Was there some kind of punishment from Source if her Angelic Divine Counterpart did not choose her? Was there some penalty in the afterlife or the next lifetime that would occur because he couldn't say yes to their union in this life? She knew Cecilia had said that they could choose anything while they were on Earth, but would something negative happen to them both once they returned to the other side? She would have to ask Henry about this as soon as she could. She turned her car around at a small viewpoint outlet and headed for the shop. It was still early, but she had a feeling Henry might be there to answer her questions.

≈

Veronica used her key to open the bookstore's front door, and Henry looked up with a start from his laptop at the main counter.

"You're here early," he said, glancing at the clock. "It's not even 9 a.m., and you don't even work today. What's –"

He stopped as the telepathic communication downloaded and he could see what Veronica had been through. He sighed.

"But you aren't giving up hope, are you?" he asked.

Veronica shrugged, tears stinging her eyes.

"What if he never remembers fully who we are to each other and the life we're here to have together?"

"He *will* remember, it will be so, it's only a matter of when and what you both do about it when he does. But you know what helps him remember sooner?"

"What?" Veronica asked, a flash of hope flowing through her.

"If you remember more. Veronica, I would recommend taking this time to become the Veronica you know you truly are in all the ways possible for you. Double your meditation time and start having those BodyTalk energy medicine healing sessions I told you about to accelerate your evolution. Continue eating organic along with the superfoods as your primary form of nourishment; in fact, start a cleanse. Make the focus mentally that wherever you don't fully love yourself that Markus is mirroring back to you, be released with the detox. Gather with your Angelic family regularly. What gifts do you want to give the world? Start bringing them into form. You can't be a bookstore cashier for life, you know," he said, winking.

Suddenly, Veronica felt lit up by his words as though every letter of them had infused her body with action and Light. Henry could not be more right. There was so much she could do to be her Angelic self more fully in form now. Because she and Markus were eternally connected, he would feel these shifts whether or not he knew what was happening. At some point, his amnesia would fade and he would remember, and even better, there was so much more for Veronica herself to discover.

"One of the key missteps that I see Angelics and humans make on Earth, Veronica, is that they're always looking to the other person to change so they can have what they want. They give their power entirely to the other. Now, of course, your power is always with you, but you know what I mean, right? They're often hanging out, waiting for the other person to offer them the job or love them back or whatever it is. That's again, victim consciousness in action. You don't need Markus to remember you, and everything you are to each other, to love him. You can love him now. And you don't even need Markus to live your best life. You can live that now, and if ever he wants to join you on the ride, he can. If he doesn't, that's okay, too. You'll meet up again in non-physical."

Veronica took some cleansing breaths while Henry spoke and she started tapping Cortices, a brain-balancing energy medicine tool Meghan had shown her the other day at work, from the BodyTalk system. Her right hand was at the back of her skull, while her left hand tapped over the top of her head, then over the center of her chest and then over her stomach, right above her navel. Then, she moved her right hand up one hand width on her head and did the same thing again, tapping over all three points and breathing as she did.

"So, does that mean I never get to have a romantic relationship then? Is that why you're still single and not with your Divine Counterpart?" Veronica hadn't meant to let that last part slip out; it merely tumbled out of her mouth. She continued tapping, now with her right hand all the way up to her forehead as her left hand tapped over her three brains, head, heart and gut.

Henry cracked up. "Well, we can talk about my love life and Divine Counterpart some other time, I think you've got enough on your plate right now. But no, your spiritual team will bring a loving partner to you that will assist you in healing and resolving the pieces that you need to work on. These won't be forever partners of course, but they're important for you on the journey forward so that you can still accomplish what you came to Earth to do. In the highest alignment with Source, both, you and your Divine Counterpart will choose one another for a romantic relationship to create more Light and healing on Earth. However, you can do this no matter what and still thrive, and even experience a real loving relationship if they're not able to choose you in this lifetime."

"But nothing will feel like it feels with him," Veronica said, tears filling her eyes again, as she shuffled her feet. She suddenly felt exhausted by the entire situation.

"That's right, nothing will feel the same as when you two unite because it's not the same. Every relationship you have has a specific energetic signature and no two are alike, and certainly, they're not like the Holy Beloved Divine Counterpart union."

"Ok, okay, I can see that. But, what about this? I know this sounds silly but let's say—worst-case scenario—Markus and I don't come together in a romantic, lifelong relationship. Do I lose *points* in the Angelic world? Is there some kind of penalty he and I receive because we didn't do it right? Like what happens at a spiritual level in all of this?"

Veronica grabbed one of the stools they used for reaching books on higher shelves and sat down on it. Henry leaned against the windowsill; his arms crossed thoughtfully.

"You ask excellent questions, Veronica." Henry said. "No, there's no penalty or points lost. But it does mean you and he will have to come back either to Earth or another obstacle-course laden world to try to unite again. Until you both choose each other and experience the radiant Light and creation that you're meant for, you will be in samsara—the cycle of life and death. This is a risk that Angelics take when they split into halves and incarnate on Earth. But even so Veronica, I wouldn't worry too much about that now. The Earth and the collective consciousness are in such a pressurized state that I sense all Divine Counterparts will come together in this lifetime."

"But what if it's like when I'm seventy or eighty and not as hot and youthful as I am now?" Veronica was exaggerating, but at the same time, it was a legitimate concern for her, even though she knew it sounded ridiculous.

Henry stood up from the windowsill and came over to Veronica, squatting down to meet her eye-to-eye. "Remember, it's your Holy Beloved Divine Counterpart. You'll look just as luscious to him as you always have and vice versa. You know, Veronica, when you're looking at another being, you aren't only seeing their physical aspects. You're seeing their Soul shining through. And I believe that at the highest level, all beings are wise beings. Besides, what if wrinkles and other 'aging' accouterments were really the Divine self, the Wise self shining through? What if we're all the Buddha wrinkled up from the inside, shining out?"

"Huh. I never, ever thought of it that way," Veronica said. "It's like those gorgeous photos you see of old women all wrinkled up but shining so bright and gorgeously happy. Hmm...what if that's the true self and the shiny 'youthful' shell is merely a mask that we have to free ourselves from and the Earthly 'aging' process allows that to happen? Whoa. I'm going to have to sit with that one, Henry. Geesh! I come to you with one question and leave with a hundred more."

"One question Veronica? Oh, it's never one question," he teased. "But that's how it works on this path, always more to discover."

Veronica sighed, tapping out her Cortices again.

"You better head home now and integrate all that you just went through, or otherwise I'm gonna put you to work," he said with a smirk.

"Yeah, yeah. I certainly have a lot of meditating to do. Thank you as always, Henry. I'm so happy my spiritual team set me up to meet you in this life and have your support on this wild journey."

"I am too," he said.

Veronica turned to leave, and as she did, Henry called out after her. "Hey, Veronica, we're meeting at my place for meditation tomorrow night as always. Be sure to come. Maybe invite Markus or something too..."

She whirled around, amused.

"Oh, great idea Henry."

He laughed. "Well, you know where to find me, I'm full of them."

CHAPTER 9

Knock, knock, knock.

Veronica sat in meditation on the floor of her bedroom beneath her unmade bed and a stack of books she had been meaning to read nearby. Rose quartz gemstone in hand, she was attempting to keep her mind in a peaceful state. It wasn't exactly working. As usual, Margot didn't wait for a reply, peaking her head into the room.

"Oops! Sorry, Ronni, just wanted to check in on you."

Veronica's eyes popped open.

"Oh, it's okay Margot, I only have thirty seconds left." She said as she held up her meditation timer. "What's up?"

"Listen, I know you don't want to talk about whatever happened with Markus, but I happened to notice that you didn't come home last night. Soooo, if by chance you *do* want to talk about it, I'm here for you." She smiled slightly and then her tone turned more serious. "And you know I'm sorry for always hassling you about changing your career and settling down with a 'good' man. I had an insight the other day as I picked up that *Life of Magic* Oracle from Dr. Strang that I told you about. Turns out, that's not necessarily the most helpful thing I could be doing as your sister."

Veronica's eyes grew big as she watched Margot step into a new level of humility, apology and openness. Henry and the other Angelics had told her that the more she aligned with who she really was, the more the people and relationships around her would self-heal or harmonize. Veronica was now seeing it in action in this very moment with Margot.

"Ah, thanks. I know your intentions are good and that you only want the best for me. I know you want me to have the kind of success and wealth you have, and I appreciate that. I'm learning now that my path is different from most and I'm learning to be okay with that, rather than analysis-paralysis myself. You know?"

Margot took a breath, placing her hand on her heart. "Yeah, you gotta live the life that calls to your heart and Soul, not the life that I or anyone else wants for you. And I'm sorry again that I haven't been as supportive of that as I could be. Is Markus part of this different-from-the-mainstream path you're feeling called to?" she asked, rather gingerly.

"Yes, get over here, I'll tell you everything!" Veronica said motioning her sister to sit down next to her on the floor.

"I want as many details as you're down to share," Margot replied, getting herself into a crossed leg position, and grabbing one of Veronica's throws off the bed to put over her.

Veronica shared with her about the dreams she had, what happened at the concert that she couldn't tell her before, and how she had met others like her through the bookstore. She shared how the bookstore and her desire to work at one was a signpost that led her to her spiritual family.

Margot was quiet for a bit, and Veronica felt a wave of nervousness move through her. She had forgotten how banana-cakes a story like this could sound to those who hadn't had these kinds of experiences in their own life.

"That doesn't mean me as your human family gets kicked to the curb, right? I'm a bit concerned Ronni that your Angelic family is going to take precedence over me. Cuz I'm kinda hoping we can stay close in this life; I mean who else is gonna take care of me when I'm old? You know I'm not about to have any kids if I can help myself."

Veronica laughed as she pulled her sister into an embrace, kissing the side of her face. "You're always my human sister, no matter what, and as long as you don't bug me too much, I promise to be here to help you out. Even when you're old and grey."

"Okay, well that's good to know," Margot said. "Just be careful with these new friends, okay? I don't want to lose you entirely."

Veronica hadn't considered that her Angelic family would be a threat to Margot and she was surprised by her sister's vulnerable reaction.

"I hear you sister, and you're not going to lose me," Veronica said putting her arm around Margot again.

"I sure hope not. I love you too much," Margot said, tears in her eyes. Blinking quickly she hurriedly changed the subject. "Alright, well, you may continue your story now."

Veronica paused, filing Margot's concern away as something to follow-up on at another time, and went on to share about the date at Salt with Markus, the night with him, the next-level make-out session, and the exquisite connection they shared, followed by the exquisite heart–she wanted to say heartbreak, but that wasn't even what it was. The pain of Markus not feeling the immediate yes for a life with her couldn't be described as heartbreak. Rather it was heart opening; even the pain was opening her. She was intent on taking seriously what Henry had shared with her. She had a responsibility as an Angelic to embody her Divine Self and live that in this incarnation–no matter if she united romantically with her Divine Counterpart or not.

"God, Ronni, that's so mature of you. So you aren't, like, angry with him? Or think he's the biggest idiot ever, or wish you had never met him? You know, like how most women would feel in your position?"

"No, weirdly, I don't. Instead, I feel this pure, big, unending Love in my heart for him. A Love that I know is eternal and will never fade. But yeah, maybe my personality does feel like he's a big idiot–I mean, a little bit." Veronica said, bringing her fingers together to show what she meant.

She and Margot howled in laughter. It felt wonderful to finally share so openly with her sister about what she had been experiencing and to have her along for the ride in this mystical adventure she was on.

"That's an understandable reaction, Ronni, even if you're embodying your Divine Angelic self. Btws, I wonder what I am...a mere human, you think?"

Veronica reflected for a bit. "I think it's obvious that you're a friend of the Angelics, and maybe even an Angelic in-training, because we did choose one another to be sisters."

"You really think we choose each other before we incarnate? Like we chose Mom and Dad and all of it?"

Veronica rolled her eyes at the mention of their mom and dad.

"Yeah, I know we chose it all before incarnating. And clearly, we chose to have absent parents so that we could lean on each other and become who we really are."

The two had leaned on each other to get through a life of parents who were busy partying and engaging in immature relationships with other immature humans. Now, their relationship with their parents was fairly neutral. Their dad lived in Scottsdale, Arizona living his dream life as a never-ending frat boy, even in his sixties. He was living his best life and Veronica was frankly happy to see it. He deserved happiness and now that he had two grown daughters, why shouldn't he? Margot was slightly more annoyed with him, but they saw him occasionally on holidays and loved going to Arizona for the warm desert sunshine.

Their mom now lived on the coast with their stepfather. She had softened in her sixties and Veronica didn't mind much having dinner here or there with them. It appeared time had calmed both of their parents down and made them slightly more available to their daughters than they were in childhood.

Their mother had apologized for all of this over a whiskey and seven one night long ago. Veronica had brushed it aside but chafed at her mother's comment that they had "done the best they could." She hadn't seen it that way. They hadn't really done anything, certainly not their best, other than keep her and Margot alive. And truth be told, it was Margot and Veronica who had helped each other thrive.

As Margot and Veronica had a laugh about their two incompetent parents, they embraced again, squeezing each other closely, grateful to have one another. Veronica could feel Margot's insecurity about her Angelic family and her desire to protect her, and she hoped that over time Margot would let it go.

"And...this is probably why Henry and Meghan were encouraging me to do some inner child work. After having this conversation with you, I agree," Veronica said. "We had a rough go of it then, and if I want to be who I truly am in this life, I'm gonna have to get on this inner child healing train. I know there's more in my subconscious around my worth and value that I need to address. You can't have the childhood we've had and not have some blockages. Maybe that's another reason why I wasn't able to take action towards my dreams until this whole spiritual awakening thing."

Margot sat thoughtfully, as she repositioned herself opposite her sister to stretch out her legs. Moving into a yogic pigeon pose, she continued, her head hanging down as she spoke. "You know that Spirit-led Oracle I shared with you? The author talks about doing inner child work too. I probably could benefit from checking that out as well. It most likely explains my romantic relationship life. I like it light and easy...oh my

God, like DAD. Like our dad. Oh no!" Margot immediately moved out of the yoga pose, sitting upright on her heels, shaking her body as if disgusted by this revelation. "I gotta reconsider hanging out with you Ronni, I think your Angelic spiritual-ness is awakening me too, and I'm not so sure I like it!" Margot stuck out her tongue at her little sister.

Veronica shook her head. "Oh my, now *that's* a revelation sister! Inner child work, here we come, eh?! I know it's not the easiest stuff, but c'mon, what else were we gonna do? Keep our heads buried in the sand and avoid looking at any of this stuff, and meanwhile, our life circumstances keep pointing towards it? It's not worth it to ignore it. Take Dad for instance. I mean, yeah, he's living a good life on the surface, but he has no intimacy or spirituality. Neither does Mom. We wouldn't want to have the kind of marriage she has with her husband now. Their way of doing things isn't going to work for our Souls, you know? Even if you're only a human or Angelic adjacent," she said as she stuck her tongue out at her sister.

"You know I'll take human over some of the other less-desirable options, you know, like reptiles. Honestly Ronni!"

Veronica high-fived her sister. "True dat," she replied. "It could be much worse, and we should probably do some exploring of the other types of beings who live on Earth, huh sis? So we can find out who you really are, too."

Margot feigned a smile. She couldn't bear to lose Veronica to the Angelics, so she was going to do what she could to keep Veronica close to her.

She tackled Veronica in a warm embrace, and the two fell backward onto the floor, laughing hysterically and feeling closer than ever.

CHAPTER 10

Veronica arrived at Henry's house with her rose quartz crystal, eager to start their group meditation. Her solo daily practice was lengthening, and she was enjoying the grounding, peace, and clarity from it. She couldn't bring herself to invite Markus to join for a variety of reasons, namely that he had bowed out of their romantic connection and she hadn't heard from him since that fateful morning at his studio. She felt completely done with humiliating herself when it came to him. And the avoidant aspect of her personality had quietly stuffed down thinking too much more about the whole ordeal, at least for the time being. Except now, Henry was clearly disappointed that Markus wasn't standing at the door with her.

"Oh, Markus isn't coming?" Henry said with a frown upon seeing her.

"Nice to see you too, Henry," Veronica said as she walked past him into the living room. She turned to him, mildly embarrassed, "I didn't invite Markus because I was immersed in long meditations and spiritual contemplation, and then I had the most amazing experience with my sister, and you know, for a few other reasons too...Anyway, Margot came in while I was meditating yesterday and we ended up having one of the most real conversations of our lives. It was wonderful. I told her everything about what I've been experiencing and going through, and she was supportive, save for a mild concern about my leaving her behind for my Angelic family." Veronica shrugged, hoping her explanation was enough, and that Henry would leave it be.

But Henry had other ideas. "And so . . . you forgot to invite your Divine Counterpart to our meditation because the rest of your life is going so well?" Henry asked with a quizzical look on his face.

Veronica awkwardly adjusted her black scoop neck tunic. "I mean, no, but yeah, I don't know. Henry, I'm really stretching myself here with all of this as it is. Inviting Markus after he said he was a 'no' for our relationship felt like too much for me to do. As you've seen, I've been super vulnerable with him and I couldn't see violating his boundary to be here tonight. I mean, I don't feel there's more I can do. Every Soul gets to choose, isn't that what you've told me? All I can do is trust at this point, while hanging on to a rapidly fraying strand of hope that he'll awaken one day and know that I'm his Holy Beloved."

Tears filled Veronica's eyes and she looked away, batting her eye lashes to make them stop. She hadn't realized that Meghan and Eric were already sitting in Henry's living room. Eric cleared his throat and Veronica startled when he did.

"Oh, hey guys! Sorry, I just unloaded all of that on you, too."

Meghan and Eric shook their heads, "No worries, Veronica, we only wanted you to know we were here before you said more. You know, in case you didn't want this to be known by us too."

"Nah, I don't care, we're all family anyway," Veronica said.

Meghan, ever the one to recalibrate the focus to the positive aspects piped in, "Who is this new Veronica? Not inviting your Divine Counterpart to meditation because too many other magical things were happening? Connecting with your human sister in a new upleveled way? Honoring Markus's boundaries and trusting that he will choose as he needs to? You're integrating into your Angelic self quite nicely, aren't you girl?!"

Veronica appreciated this reflection from Meghan because she wasn't exactly feeling like she was rocking her Angelic life, especially with Markus flat out refusing to move forward with her. Meghan was right that she had changed in many ways already. If she didn't think about Markus, she did feel more relaxed, more accepting, and more at peace. Her talk with Henry and with Margot had really helped her out too.

"Well, I have the best idea anyway for Veronica's Divine Counterpart situation," Edward said as he and Cecilia walked in from the kitchen with a tray of mason jars filled with hibiscus ice tea for everyone, having clearly overheard their conversation. Veronica burst into a full-body laugh; she loved having such support from her Angelic family.

"Oh, do tell," Veronica said, dropping herself onto a cushion in front of the leather sofa.

"Yes, do tell," Cecilia said, shaking her head and giggling as she sat down on the leather couch across from Veronica, her infamous copper bracelets jingling as she adjusted herself into a comfortable position. "This is the first I've heard about this."

"Tonight, after our meditation, let's all send love and healing vibrations to Markus," said Edward as he placed the tray of ice teas on the coffee table in the center of the room and grabbed his meditation cushion, placing it on the floor next to Cecilia. "We'll make it like a healing, for him and Veronica. Let's send through the ethers that he awakens more fully as an Angelic and sees who Veronica truly is to him."

"Well honey, that's a lovely idea," Cecilia said, patting his shoulder.

Meghan and Eric were snuggled up on the floor together, sitting on cushions with a red throw blanket over their legs. Meghan clapped her hands together and cheered, and Eric responded heartily with a yes as well.

Henry spoke up next. "Edward, that's perfect. Why haven't we been doing that after every meditation for those we wish to see awaken? This is brilliant. I am in." He scanned the room. "Everyone else in too?"

Everyone nodded, and Veronica felt so much gratitude for her Angelic family.

"You all are amazing. I could not have hoped for or asked for a better Angelic family. Thank you, this means so much to me. And of course, no attachment, but it will be interesting to see if Markus feels anything or what might transpire afterwards."

Henry rubbed his palms together, "Indeed it will be. Are we ready, family?"

Everyone settled into their positions in Henry's living room, including Henry in his luxuriously oversized white chair that he loved to meditate in. White tealight candles were placed throughout the living room and Cecilia hopped off the couch to dim the overhead lights to set the mood.

Veronica entered the meditation earnest for the possibilities that lay ahead. Henry reminded everyone that they would spend thirty-three minutes focused on their breath while also allowing whatever guidance or wisdom from the Light that wanted to present to them to be made known. They all had notebooks next to them this time to jot down any insights or unique guidance that came through. If stories or narratives came through from their life, they were to keep their focus fixed on their breath, not giving energy to anything that wasn't of the Light. And of course, they would start the thirty-three minutes with several rounds of inhaling up what no longer served them to carry and exhaling it out of their mouth until they could move into a peaceful state where greater wisdom could come through.

"Once the timer goes off after thirty-three minutes, Edward, would you guide us through the prayer and intention for Markus?"

Edward agreed, and Meghan quickly jumped up from where she was laying with Eric to give Veronica a hug. Eric smiled over at them and Veronica had the feeling of being genuinely held and loved by a family unit. Perhaps for the first time in her life.

The meditation was luscious for Veronica. She felt herself drop into an unlimited place of no real thought and instead enjoyed the feelings of lightness and full presence. She didn't have images or guidance come to her, as sometimes others did, and it didn't even occur to her to want that. She simply wanted to feel unified with the Light, the true essence of herself and all sentient beings. And that was exactly what she got to experience.

As the timer dinged that the thirty-three minutes was over, Veronica yawned and stretched her body out first upwards towards the sky and then forwards, placing her legs out in front of her and stretching fully. Her body felt so good to her now, no longer heavy or dense; she instead felt light and supple. As she stretched, it was as if the heavenly energy she was experiencing was grounding into her body.

Edward then spoke. "Alright family, let's picture Markus in our mind's eye. I believe we all know what he looks like after Veronica showed us his website featuring his photograph the other day."

Veronica and Meghan giggled at this and Cecilia could be heard lightly slapping Edward's shoulder as she tried to hold back a laugh. Edward took a deep breath, a broad smile on his face palpable through his voice. "Hold the image of Markus strongly in your mind, and as we do this together, we activate his image clearly in our collective Angelic mind. I'll give you a minute or so to do this."

This was easy-peesy for Veronica as over these last few months there was never a time that Markus's image wasn't with her. She pulled him up in her mind's eye, seeing his sparkling blue eyes, brown skin, curly hair, and toned physique before her. Her heart softened at the sight of him and an Immense Love filled her very being.

"Now, send the phrase 'You are Loved' to Markus. Let him feel how loved and celebrated he is by the Angelic Realm. Beam the phrase 'You are Loved' over and over to him. I'll give us all a few minutes to do this."

Edward knew that the collective power of their Angelic family could reach Markus, but that this only truly worked because Markus was Veronica's Divine Counterpart. If they had tried to do this for any boyfriend or any ole connection of hers or for anyone, it would have very little if any impact. It was the Sacred Holy Union of Markus and Veronica that made this possible and the gathering of their Angelic family with this focus, that accelerated and exponentiated the impact.

"Next, send Markus the image of him and Veronica together, united in Sacred Holy Union. Perhaps you send him images of their sacred ceremony, or perhaps you send him images of the two of them together in life. Use your intuitive knowing to guide you."

Instantly, Veronica saw her Sacred Union Ceremony with Markus. She saw them outside, in a rose garden of some sort, with her in a beautiful blush gown, him in linen and with a full beard. His eyes were watering as she walked towards him and they embraced, while the brightest sunshine beamed down upon them and all around. In this image, it was only the two of them, and she could hear the coo-ing of peace doves as well as the chickadees chirping. She could even smell the late summer and early fall scents in the garden of rose and lilac. She felt an incredibly celebratory energy with them and a love so deep it burned throughout her every cell. She held this image and sent it to Markus, feeling such overwhelming (in the best way) Immense Love within her as she did.

"Now Angelic family, we'll close out this time focused on Markus with a chant that we'll send him with ease, 'M & V, together for eternity. M & V, together for eternity. M & V, together for eternity. We want to flood his consciousness with the remembrance of his holy, Divine agreement in this incarnation with Veronica."

Although Veronica was certain that Edward meant they would do this silently, slowly she heard them all softly chanting the mantra, "M & V, together for eternity. M & V, together for eternity."

After several minutes of this, Edward said, "And so it is. It is SO. It is done. It is complete." Then he placed his hands in a prayer position and offered it up to the sky.

"You may open your eyes whenever you feel ready," Henry said after a few minutes.

When Veronica opened her eyes, she thought for a moment that she saw Markus standing right in front of her. The image was so real, it startled her and she jumped her whole body back onto the couch that she had been leaning against. Meghan came over quickly, and clamped her hand on Veronica's arm to ground her. "What did you see?" she said.

"I ... I don't know. It startled me. I opened my eyes and thought that I saw Markus right in front of me. It was so real, it just, it caught me off guard. Did any of you have an experience like that??"

No one said anything for a minute and Veronica began tapping her Cortices to rebalance her energy.

Finally, Cecilia spoke, "Our collective energy of Love and images of you and Markus together activated a quantum leap in the timeline, Veronica. This was a powerful healing transformation that took place here tonight. I'm not surprised you saw him. I don't know that any of us would have that experience because he is *your* Divine Counterpart and our focus was simply speeding up what The Divine has already outlined for you both."

"Do you mean that tonight we interfered in his natural process?" Veronica wasn't clear on exactly what Cecilia was saying and worried that perhaps they had done something they shouldn't have.

"All beings have free will, and even your own Angels on your spiritual team in non-physical can't interfere in your life trajectory," Cecilia said. "Because you're Markus's Divine Counterpart, you can nudge him and as his spiritual family we can nudge him to remember what he already planned for himself. He can always use his free will to work against the Divine hand, but of course, our intent and prayer is that he will work in harmony with it. That's why we started with sending him the knowledge that he is Loved. If a being remembers how Loved they are—they will begin to remember other aspects of their Divine life plan and destiny. Love is who all Angelics and humans are at the core, so that's why we always start there."

Veronica sighed audibly. At this point, she had given this thing with Markus her best shot. She had done everything a woman could do to allow her Sacred Union with him to take place. Now, she would have to surrender and trust Divine forces for the next steps.

Markus was having dinner with his mother at Meridian Restaurant and Bar overlooking the Pacific Ocean, dining on pan seared halibut when he began to feel something he had never felt before. It was as if waves of energy were lapping up all around him. It was not unpleasant, but it was distracting.

"And then I said to Sheila, 'Listen, I can't help it if my son is a mega-watt star and yours can't get out from in front of those video games. Don't be angry with me.' You know how persnickety she can be, always making everything a competition," Judy, Markus's mother said.

His mother, a petite woman with a bottle-blonde, curly bob and sparkling blue eyes—that Markus clearly got from her—was chatting his ear off all night about some silly row she had with one of her cousins, over Markus's fame. While she preferred to act annoyed by all the attention she got as famous Markus's mother and all the envy it drew from her extended family, she secretly, or not-so-secretly relished it. The problem now was, Markus was fully unable to indulge her storyline and began speaking as she continued to rattle on.

"Mother, I'm sorry, but I'm not feeling so good right now. I think I need to go home and rest," Markus said.

"Oh honey, are you okay? Are you sick?" she asked.

"I don't know. I feel strange, almost like an enormous wave of energy is washing over me. I think I need to go lay down," he said.

"I wonder if it was the fish?" she asked.

"I don't know, it doesn't feel like a stomach thing, it's more like an all around my body thing," Markus extended his arms all around him to illustrate.

His mother pursed her lips together in concern but decided that pressing him more on the topic would be moot. Ever the caretaker, she said, "I'll put the rest of your dinner into a to-go box and will bring it by later tonight. You go now, and I'll wrap up everything here."

Thankfully the drive to Markus's home wasn't far and within ten minutes of feeling the strange sensations, Markus climbed the stairs to his flannel covered bed to lie down. It was the only position that felt comfortable, as he felt the waves of energy pulsing continually around him.

He found himself drifting into a meditative, lucid-dream-like state where he was surrounded by a mass of Angels, glowing gold, white and pink. He was in the center, witnessing their presence. As he did, a deluge of what could only be described as unconditional love flooded his being-ness, so much so, tears sprang from his eyes. Never had he felt so loved.

In this dream-like state, he was lying on a healing table as the Angels surrounded him, and one Angel came up to him, placing her hands on his heart. He cried even more as he raised his head and saw her face. It was Veronica. Veronica. While he had put her off in the physical plane because his feelings for her were far too overwhelming for his physical life unfolding, here it was different.

All he felt for her upon seeing her face was an overflowing Immense Love. It was her. He reached up to touch her face, his fingers present to how her angelically soft, radiant skin felt in the dream state. He then moved his hand to her heart, and she placed her other hand over his.

As he did this, he was catapulted to a scene, in the forest or maybe a garden. He and Veronica stood before one another in a sacred ceremony. Wearing a flowing, strapless blush gown that flowed into the grass, Veronica glowed. He saw himself wearing linen pants and a blush shirt, a full beard on his face. He was both in the scene and watching the scene from another vantage point.

Warm rays of sunlight beamed down upon them and he could not get over how stunningly gorgeous she was, her long curls cascading down her shoulders, her buttery skin glowing with a dew that looked like an angelic mist upon a human body. He felt the rightness in their union and the blessing of Source upon them in coming together.

The scene didn't last long, and next thing he knew, he was back in the healing space, this time all the Angels gathered closer in around him as they chanted a chant he could not clearly hear. All that remained was him peering into Veronica's eyes, their hands on one another's hearts. Pink and golden light swirled around them, and after some time, he closed his eyes and drifted into a deep, deep sleep.

It was several hours later when Markus awoke, the skies dark and a sliver of moonlight bathing his bedroom floor. He felt as though he had slept an entire lifetime and sat up on his bed, trying to remember what had happened. Slowly he recounted feeling woozy at dinner with his mom and her hurriedly sending him off to return home. Then he saw her face. Veronica. The remnants of the dream returned and chills covered his body. He wasn't sure exactly what was going on, and he stood up to head downstairs to the kitchen to grab a glass of water.

Upon standing, he immediately sat back down, he felt so off balance. He tried again, this time taking full breaths and feeling his feet (a trick a cranial-sacral healer had shown him long ago) so that he could ground himself more into his body. Had he experienced some kind of healing event? He had endured intense fevers in the past or a sickness that seemed to purge his body of toxins. But this was not that. This was like some kind of spiritual remembering and it was linked to Veronica.

He ran his hands over his now messy and unmade bed, letting the texture of the fabric bring him more into his body. Shaking his head, he realized he would not be able to avoid thinking more intently about his connection with Veronica any longer. Here it was, what he had prayed to God for long ago. What he had believed in. His Divine Counterpart, and when faced with that possibility he was a coward. He was afraid. So much so that he attempted to cling to the life that had defined him as a "famous" musician.

It was a life that his Soul had become weary of, but which his ego clearly couldn't let go of. Of course, he knew that if he didn't let go of it when Divinely shown to do so, that a more dramatic letting go would happen at the hands of Divine providence. At thirty-four, he hadn't lived aligned with every spiritual principle, but he knew this one to be true. You either followed the guidance you had asked for and were blessed with, or you didn't and it was a bumpier ride that eventually landed you with a thud right where you needed to be.

He recalled the time he ignored specific guidance that he had received some fifteen years earlier in a dream and how he had refused it. At that time, he was shown a theater to buy and renovate, where he would nurture new artists and The Sunshine State would hold shows regularly. While this would have been a wonderful expansion for any musician, he couldn't shake the desire to be more famous and successful, like Grammy's and Music Hall of Fame success. Ironically the family who had ended up taking over the theater hit gold, and created a name for themselves as famous artists, plays and events came to them. If Markus had followed his dream, he possibly could have hosted a Music Hall of Fame event there. Because of this error, it was six months before he was blessed with another prophetic dream after that. It was agonizing for him to have been abandoned by his dreamtime guidance, and Markus knew he had caused it, for he had failed to honor the Divine guidance given to him.

Markus did not want this to be another one of those times. He would always end up where The Divine desired for him to be, knowing that he was The Divine in form, so this was not a plan that was outside of him, but rather The Divine plan he had created for his lifetime before incarnating. He would get there one way or the other, whether in this lifetime or the next. It was far easier to go with it and work *with* the guidance than to resist or ignore it and have to reincarnate and do it all again, hoping he would make the right choice when given the opportunity. The dream imagery and sensations he was having were showing him what Markus had known within his psyche but had been ignoring and too afraid to honor. Something about whatever he had just gone through was making all of this crystal clear to him with absolute ease.

Untangling from his record label would be tricky. But if he stayed, he would continue molding his music to their controlled desires. His relationships would have to be approved by them, and his life would not be fully his own. In fact, he needed to get back to Katie about setting up a date with Isabel. What would happen if he backed out of all of it? Based on what Mr. Schwan had told him, if he retracted, things would not go well for him.

Then, there was Veronica. It seemed as though she was the answer to what he had experienced long ago as a boy. Their path together was the path he should take, now as a man. But did he have the courage to finally take it? Something Markus had told no one–not even his mother whom he was close to–was that he had a profound dream as a little boy. A wise Angelic being had come to him in his dream state and told him that he too was an Angel, upon Earth. He was told that his life would come into its highest form upon uniting with his Holy Beloved. A girl he had only seen from behind in his dream state, and that he could recognize by the black curls upon her head.

Markus leaned his head back and said out loud to his Angelic family and Source HerSelf, "Thank you. Please give me the courage to follow my highest path. And so it is. It is so."

CHAPTER 11

Veronica paced Secret Beach, barely aware of the sparkling, lapping waves and broken shells along the water's edge. On one hand, her life was better than it had ever been since the Markus-dream-spiritual-awakening. She knew for the first time in her life why she was the way she was– aka, quirky and not in alignment with the mainstream. This made her love herself more than she ever had. Her early childhood desire for a Soul-based love now made sense, not to mention her dream of owning a bookstore. Of course, the bookstore was how she would meet her Angelic family, so that's why her desire for it had been so strong for so long! She and her sister Margot were closer than ever, and even though Margot had some concerns about the new path she was on, mostly she was inspired by it, and Veronica was so grateful for what was unfolding between them. Even her long-time friend Eloise, while utterly confused about what was happening in Veronica's life, loved her and let her know she would always be there for her. On top of that, Veronica was in the best physical health of her life.

And then there was Markus. Her Divine Counterpart, the Soul connection she knew existed as a child, who basically spat in her face. He felt the connection, knew it was special and important *and* was a hard no for doing anything about it. She had given their connection everything she could, and still it didn't seem to matter to him.

Her recycled light blue and pink Nikes pounded the sand as her mind attempted to make sense of how her life could be good in so many ways while at the same time, one of the most important pieces could be so far out of place. It had been almost two hours of pacing the beach like this and she wasn't finding clarity. The only thing that kept ringing in her ears was to continue moving forward, one foot in front of the other. As she headed back to her car, a couple and their two twin girls with ebony pigtails and bright pink sand buckets walked onto the beach, a picnic basket in tow.

That's what I want to have with Markus, she heard a whisper inside of her say. She turned around swiftly to see who had said such a thing. She hadn't consciously thought she wanted children, but...

For now, she would have to add this to the almost toppling pile of magic that was her connection with Markus Mullins.

Making her way up the stairs to Margot's house, her purple workout pants and white tank now clinging to her, she thought she heard the faint sounds of a blender coming from inside. She checked her phone as she opened the front door. It was 2 p.m. and Margot was usually at work at this time.

Sure enough the Vita-Mix was blaring, on high-speed no less.

"Margot—"

She had caught her in the act. There stood Margot, in her charcoal grey blouse and black bell bottom slacks and heels, her hair in a French twist making herself one of Veronica's PowerShakes.

Margot's eyes widened, "Shit, I thought you were gonna be gone longer."

"Gimme, that!" Veronica said playfully lunging at her sister's pink Yeti mug.

"Hey! Remember I was the one who gave you the bag of this first, it was mine initially. I just took pity on your poor, couldn't-get-over Ben soul and gave it to you."

Veronica scoffed. "Give me a break. You only want this now because I Love it."

"Well, that's true," Margot said with a laugh. "But you already had one today and well, you were right, this is really, really good."

"What happened to already being perfect?" Veronica said, as she began to make her second PowerShake of the day.

"Perfection can always be improved upon," Margot said, placing her arm around Veronica. "Eww...you're sweaty."

"Yeah, that's what happens when you spend a couple of hours pacing Secret Beach in a fruitless search for meaning."

"So, no word from Markus yet?"

"As if there would be, the guy said he couldn't do it. It's been two weeks, obviously he meant it." Veronica poured the PowerShake into the stainless-steel tumbler she had received with her last Purium order. "Did you put the scoop of MVP Family chocolate in it?"

Margot nodded.

"And a small handful of organic frozen berries?"

Margot nodded again.

"Damn sister, you've been watching me and taking notes. How long have you been making your own shakes without my knowing?"

Margot paused, pretending to try to remember. Veronica swatted at her and she leaned away, moving over to sit at the dining table.

"Don't deflect Ronni, I know this is hard for you, the Markus thing I mean. And I'm sure it didn't help with me questioning you about your Angelic family too."

Veronica walked over to where her sister was, sitting down

at the dining room table as she took a drink of her shake, "I mean, I know that ultimately you love me and will have my back, you and Eloise are good like that. But the Markus thing is gut-wrenching when I let myself think too much about it. I mean, this whole awakening only started because of him, and he's the one aspect of my life that has totally tanked. Or I should say flatlined before it even got started. It doesn't make any sense. I know he has free will and he's using it to choose gorgeous models and actresses to be with, but come, on. Can't I catch a break?!"

Margot leaned over, rubbing Veronica's back. "It will all become clear soon Ronni. Give it some time. It's usually when we're on the other side of the mess that we can see why it all happened and what it means."

Veronica shrugged, "I sure hope so sis, cuz it sucks right now."

"Hey, listen, I know what will cheer you up. How about we play another round of 'Margot's great business ideas for Ronni' brought to you by Big Sister Knows Best?"

Veronica laughed. "Oh good, my favorite game. But, remember what the Oracle said?"

"I know, I know, so that's why this one is easy. It's pretty obvious honestly," Margot said as she titled her head all the way back drinking the last of her PowerShake. "You're absolutely in love with these superfoods and they have an affiliate program you could join, become a brand partner for them and work that biz while you work at the bookstore with your Angelic peeps. You get to do both, increase your income, and you could be like, I don't know, the superfoods queen on the Oregon Coast."

Veronica had to admit it wasn't a bad idea.

"You know, I *am* in love with the way the superfoods make my body feel. I feel lighter, I have more energy, and I'm sleeping better. Doesn't do me a ton of good without Markus, but hey, it's still a win. I did see that their superfoods are grown in regenerative soil and the packaging is all compostable, which is the wave of the future. Maybe I could even have their Juice-Bar-In-A-Bag juices available at my bookstore."

"Plot twist. What? Are you thinking you're finally ready to make a move on having your own bookstore? Will it compete with Henry?" Margot had moved beyond surprised and into straight shock.

"I'm going to talk to him about possibilities because I absolutely would *not* be in competition with him. Maybe like a franchise thing? Up the Coast or down near the Cali border for that matter?" Veronica said.

"Yeah, that's a great idea! And maybe this is how you bring in your millions–to pay for your bookstore–with the Purium superfoods?"

"That would be a great way for me to generate extra cash flow for setting up my own shop. Hmm...something to think about. Maybe I've been sitting on a gold mine here with you. I should probably just go ahead and hire you as my business manager to work out all the details," Veronica said as she headed over to the sink to rinse out her mug.

Margot followed her. "Well, I'm *very* expensive, but I've got no problem giving my little sis some help along the way. Believe it or not, though, I do have something else to talk to you about other than superfoods and other cushy biz ideas. Like, your hot body. Ronni, Damn! I've never seen you so fit, your body is super-hot sis."

"Nice side benefit, eh?" Veronica said, shaking her butt at her sister.

Margot agreed, scanning Veronica from head to toe. "I don't believe the world has ever seen a Ronni like this!" she said with a playful slap of her sister's behind.

"Okay, but seriously, what's up, what else did you want to chat me up about, besides my super-hot superfoods body and of course to hammer me with more sisterly suggestions?" said Veronica.

"Weeelllll...I'm not sure how this going to land now, but I

did just find out some interesting news. Turns out your boy Markus is going to be playing a show this weekend at the Aladdin Theater in Portland. Remember when we saw India Arie there, and she saged the whole stage like the goddess she is? Anyway, I would love to take you to the show, especially since we haven't been to the Aladdin in so long. We could have Eloise come with us too and have a fun girl's night. It would all be my treat. He wouldn't even have to know we were there; he's got a guy Adam-somebody opening who's supposed to be really great too. We'll just enjoy the music. Maybe it can even be like a reset from the first concert, bringing it full circle, only this time you don't have a spiritual awakening where you remember you love him. What do you say?"

Veronica loved the idea of seeing Markus play again, but there was no way her heart could handle seeing him so soon. She could barely listen to his music since their last conversation. Besides it seemed a tad aggressive to show up at one of his concerts.

"Uh sis, read the room. No way. Don't get me wrong, having a girl's night with you and Eloise in Portland sounds like a blast. However, I would most definitely be entering stalker territory if I came to his concert without having heard from him. But what if you and Eloise went and did some re-con for me to find out wtf is going on with him? I'm joking. Mostly."

Margot frowned. "Shoot. I knew it might be too far out there for you, but when I saw he was playing I thought it was worth a shot. But yeah, you're right. You can't just show up if he isn't communicating with you. But, I mean, you guys are friends, though, no matter what, right? So it wouldn't be like a total stalker sitch..." Her voice trailed off and she quickly grabbed her phone.

"Don't even think about it, Margot, I'm not going. But it's okay if you go, his music *is* actually fantastic. Thanks for trying to cheer me up and for thinking of me," Veronica hollered as she headed to her room to shower so she could meet up with her Angelic family for a bonfire at Nye Beach.

As she towel dried her hair, Veronica felt lighter, like she had washed off some of the heaviness that had been weighing on her about Markus from her time at Secret Beach. She hummed along to the sounds of the 432hz healing music that Meghan and Eric had turned her onto. There were hours upon hours of healing nature sounds on YouTube and she found herself listening to it a lot over the past two weeks.

Her phone pinged and she was shocked to see that it was a text from Markus. Were his ears burning after her and Margot's conversation about him?

"Hey V, I know it's been a minute, but I would like to talk to you. I have a show happening this weekend in Portland at the Aladdin–would you be down to be my guest & then we could spend some time after to talk? I can leave two tickets for you at will call if you wanna bring a friend."

Veronica scowled. She didn't know whether to be excited or frightened. What were the odds of Margot roughly an hour earlier asking her to go to this same show? Veronica took a deep breath, tapped out her Cortices, and placed both hands on her heart. She imagined going to his concert and asked her heart how that felt. Lightness, joy, and love rushed over her. Veronica imagined staying home for the weekend, working extra hours at the shop, and avoiding the show. She felt heavy and sick to her stomach. So. That was all she needed to know. Veronica texted him back to let him know she'd be there and she'd bring Margot too. She hit send and then went searching for Margot.

"Margot, where are you? I have some slightly strange but I think good news."

Margot seemed to magically appear from the living room.

"Oh hey, what?" she said, acting sort of odd.

"What's going on? Why are you being so weird?" Veronica said, noticing something felt off with the way her sister was behaving.

"Oh, nothing Ronni. I'm waiting to hear back from a potential buyer for a multi-million-dollar listing. You know that always puts me a little on edge," Margot said, shaking her head, as though trying to shake off her nerves.

"Okay, well, I guess that makes sense. Hey, listen, weird turn of events. Markus just texted to say he wants to talk to me, and would I meet him after his show this weekend in Portland. He said he would leave two tickets for me at will call if I wanted to bring someone. So bizarro, right?"

"Or...total Divine synchronicity that you should follow?!" Margot asked.

"Yeah, or that." Veronica smirked. "Anyway, do you want to go with me? And maybe we can get a ticket for Eloise or even Ryan too, so I don't blow you off after when I go talk with Markus?"

"I'm definitely taking that second ticket. I wonder where he'll give us seats at...But, um, I'm kinda over Ryan right now, so I'll reach out to one of my agents or friends in P-town. You could let Eloise know to meet us there if she wanted too. Anyway, don't worry about me–I'll take care of myself after the show so you and Markus can have time together."

"Depending on where his head is at, it may be a very short conversation, or of course in my best-case scenario, it could be another night with him," Veronica said wistfully.

While she would have loved to have been unattached to her outcomes with Markus, this recent interaction with him, followed by the new development of seeing him in Portland, had her anxious. Would her desired outcome take place? Or would she fly solo for this incarnation, calling in a Great Love fill-in for the Divine Counterpart who did not choose her in this life? There was nothing she could do to hurry the week along, so she would have to continue taking one day at a time, praying for the Highest Divine Will to happen in her life. That, and tapping a lot of Cortices.

~

That was a close one. Markus ran his fingers through his tousled curls. He slammed his phone down on the bed, pacing the creaky hardwood floors in his large Victorian home. After a few paces, he shuffled over to the window overlooking the bay and sighed. He hadn't put as much thought as he should have into getting Veronica to the show. Until he got her sister's "I'm-not-happy-with-you-and-stop-being-a-typical-man-jerk-text" that is.

"Markus! You haven't reached out to Ronni since the last time you saw her??! You know the time when you told her you didn't want to be with her?? Yet you expect me to get her to the show to see you? C'mon man, you gotta do better than this. She's refusing to show up like some stalker to your concert without having heard from you. So if you really want me to get her there, you're gonna have to reach out to her yourself. I don't think it blows your cover if she knows the tickets are coming from you, anyway. It'll probably make her feel special rather than thinking her sister is footing the bill. Your move, dude. –Margot"

Markus shook his head. These Walter women were not to be messed with. He should have anticipated Veronica's reaction. What an ass he was. He took a long breath, knelt on the ground, and offered up a prayer to the heavens.

"God, guide and direct my steps. May the Highest Divine Will take place between Veronica and me. Please give me the eyes to see and ears to hear so that I may fulfill my mission here on Earth."

With that, he heard a ping on his phone and was relieved to receive a text from Veronica letting him know she would be there. Now, he needed to get to work on his next steps so that he would be ready when he saw her.

~

A huge shipment of metaphysical books had arrived at the store and Veronica was elated. She had the shop all to herself for the day, and those were the days she loved the most. She enjoyed working with Henry and Meghan, but when she was alone, she could pretend it was her store. It made her savor the customer interactions, taking inventory, and cataloguing new books into their computer system even more. Veronica occasionally suggested books for Henry to carry and it thrilled her that he had ordered all of Dr. Strang's books for their channeled books section.

Veronica was on her third Oracle, *Live Like You're On Vacation,* and was devouring the wisdom on how to live a richer and more spacious life. She realized that her vibration determined the amount of abundance that flowed to her or not, and she was eager to see what might come to her as she implemented the guidance contained within the book. Each morning she "randomly" opened to a page to see what her message for the day was.

Today she had opened to this Oracle message and she could hardly believe it:

"Your Destiny shifts because now you can ascend to a greater level of spiritual understanding in your day-to-day life and now what comes to you changes in form. And we will keep it to this for now, but you will now begin to notice what we mean. Your attachment is different, your understanding is different, your desire is different, because you are here now. You are here in this place of knowing what Source knows–you heard us right–and you are in a body. And you in service to You and therefore to the All-That-Is-ness that expands and transforms and you are still and quiet and silent and filled with waves of bliss pouring over your body and tears filling your eyes and you dance with the magic that is this life. That is what you're here to do, you know this, do you not? Dance with the Magic that is this life. And in doing that, you are served and All-That-Is is served by you. And so it is. It is so."

She took pulling this message today as a reminder to detach from what Markus chose to do with their connection and to enjoy the stillness and quiet she was experiencing through her meditation practice (now up to 44 minutes) as well as her time in nature. She needed to continue to release her attachment to the outcomes, while enjoying the present moment. It seemed as though every day the reading that she "randomly" pulled was filled with the exact message she needed.

CHAPTER 12

The day of Markus's show at the Aladdin Theater arrived and Veronica woke up with what she could only describe as catastrophic anxiety. Out of nowhere, she found herself flooded with fear, doubt, and absolute uncertainty. Gripping her rose quartz crystal as though it were a lifeline, Veronica lay paralyzed in her bed as her mind crafted a litany of unanswerable questions.

How was she going to survive her life if Markus maintained his stance that all he wanted was a friends-only relationship with her? Or what if he just wanted casual sex and hook-ups and chose to ignore their spiritual assignment with one another? How was she going to be calm and grounded for the day when all she really wanted to do was fast forward to after the show to know where his heart stood? And however would she explain to him that she was an Angelic and so was he? As these thoughts engulfed her once peaceful mind, Margot knocked on her bedroom door.

"It's the big day!" Margot sing-songed from behind the closed door. Margot was now waiting until Veronica gave her the a-okay to come in before opening the door in her efforts to be more respectful of Veronica. Veronica continued to marvel at the way their relationship was upleveling since her awakening journey began.

"Come in," Veronica called from her bed. Sitting up, she pushed her curls out of her face, reached for an elastic off of her nightstand, and tied her hair up into a big knot on the top of her head. She kicked off a few of the books that were scattered on her bed, as she had tried to distract herself the night before with some romance reads. But to no avail. "By the way, why are you so cheery? It's not like it's my wedding day. And I feel so anxious, almost to the point of throwing up. What if he gives me the same song and dance–both literally and figuratively–about being friends? Or worse, he just wants a hook up-only scenario? Can I seriously handle that??"

Margot sat down on the bed with Veronica, grabbing her sister's hands accidentally knocking the rose quartz into Veronica's lap. "First of all, you can handle anything. Do you remember our childhood? Do you remember Ben falling in love with his bestie that you used to hang out with? Remember that time you tried to force yourself to work at OregonNow with its corporatized ogre leadership? Markus Mullins has *nothing* on this. Whatever he chooses says everything about the kind of man he is and is not based on whether you're 'good enough' for him or not. Okay? We're going to have a fun drive up there, we're gonna go out to dinner at that organic restaurant Harlow that you wanted to try and Eloise is going to meet us there, and we'll have a blast no matter what. OK?"

It warmed Veronica's heart how endearing and supportive Margot was being throughout all of this. Before, Margot practically had a Ph.D. in tough love, always encouraging Veronica to suck it up and move forward. Now, she was softer, gentler, and kinder, while still encouraging her to move forward.

"Thanks, Margot, that helps a lot. I'm definitely seeing some of my old wounds around worthiness showing up in this whole thing with Markus. From what we went through with mom and dad, from previous heartbreaks, from not being as fabulous as my big sister, you know that kind of stuff. I want to do some healing on it, and Henry has been telling me about this BodyTalk modality that could help me."

Margot listened closely as Veronica spoke, gently caressing her sister's hand, "Yeah, the worthiness thing *is* a thing for all of us Ronni. I've got my own ish from the pressure to continue to be this fabulous," Margot said with a chuckle. "Do you remember that author who wrote the Oracle I told you about? She also has a self-healing system called the *SuperPowers Guide* that you can use to take 'unworthiness' through. It's a five-step process that clears out and heals limiting beliefs, fears, and traumas. I've been using it lately, and it's been super helpful. You can buy it off her site and have it as quickly as right now—you could even do a session on yourself with it before we leave later today."

Veronica knew immediately that this was what she needed. "Omg, I'm on it. Text me the link right now. And look at you Margot–doing your own self-healing work? That's impressive."

"You got it sis. And yeah, what can I say, Ronni? You inspired me to go deeper. If my sister is an Angelic, I better figure out what the f I'm doing here in this life, so we can still track together. Can't have you leaving me in the evolutionary dust," she said with a wink.

She then picked up her phone, and not even a minute later Margot announced, "Incoming!" and Veronica's phone pinged.

"What did we do before all of this technology?" Veronica said as she signed up for the *SuperPowers Guide* from her bed.

Margot stood up, smoothing her pinstripe skirt, which she had paired with a silky cream blouse. Her perfectly coiffed blonde blow-out brushed against her shoulders. As per usual, she looked both professional and sophisticated, with a slight touch of sexy. "I'm headed to the office to do a signing and then I'll be out front to pick you up at 2 p.m., okay?"

"Oh yeah, are you closing that multi-million-dollar deal

today? Is that why you look extra gorgeous for work?" Veronica had been so wrapped up in all her life changes that she hadn't asked her sister about hers.

"You know it, Ronni. And thanks for noticing my extra-extra-hotness today," Margot said as she blew her sister a kiss.

"Congrats, Margot! You're seriously the most successful, baddest-ass real estate broker on the Oregon Coast."

Margot pretended to blush. "You know I am," she said breathlessly, as though she were a modern-day Marilyn Monroe. And then she was off.

~

Whoa. That SuperPowers Guide *was out-of-this-world.*

It astonished Veronica how easy and effective the *SuperPowers Guide* had been in releasing the fear and uncertainty she was feeling about what would happen between her and Markus. With pen and paper in hand, she sat on her bed, still in her cream and pink striped tank top and drawstring bottom pajamas, to dig into the healing work. She took, "I'm not lovable" through the five-step process and was stunned by the inner child work that was needed as well as the karmic deactivation from many lifetimes of carrying this wound.

The guide suggested using the five-step healing process for anyone with whom one had difficulty, so she applied it to Markus. That way, if there were any past-life interferences, they could be cleared and Veronica could show up to his concert grounded and at peace with whatever the outcome was. She did as the guide instructed and wrote out his entire name in her journal, in quote marks. She used quote marks because, as Dr. Strang explained, names are simply the roles we play in each incarnation. They're not the full truth of who a Soul is. She began releasing anything she was carrying about Markus that was not serving her, as well as integrating into her heart her little girl who wanted to be chosen—which again would act as a repellant to her Divine Counterpart saying "yes" to her.

The biggest surprise for Veronica was the karmic deactivation healing with Markus. There were many, many, *many* lifetimes of them trying to be together, coming close to being together, but then something would happen that would tear them apart. Veronica even had images of a lifetime where she drowned as they were sailing on a large ship after finally coming back to one another. She also saw another lifetime in her mind's eye where they had lived together in a fairly peaceful life as husband and wife, with a daughter, the woman who was now his mother in this lifetime. But then, an army attacked their village and their family was split apart. Tears streamed down Veronica's face as she connected to these past lifetimes with Markus's Soul and then deactivated them. She revoked all consent to carry that pain and wounding from other lifetimes with him into the present. Doing this opened her to a lifetime of joy, love, and togetherness.

By the time her sister showed up at two, Veronica felt like a new woman. She jumped into Margot's black Audi S7 and immediately admired her sister. Margot looked beautiful in her indigo blue jeans and creamy button-up blouse carried over from her work outfit earlier that day. The buttons on her blouse were left open, revealing a tasteful amount of her décolletage. Her hair was swept up in a simple updo, a few strands carefully untucked. Even from work to the concert—she was stunning.

Margot noticed Veronica checking her out and returned the favor. "You're seriously glowing, Ronni. How many SGs did you do and how many PowerShakes did you have today? My God, girl, you look radiant!"

Veronica held up two fingers on each hand and let out a voracious celebratory cheer.

"Two and two, baby. And thanks Margot for noticing. I did two SGs, and they were *so* powerful. I cleared my unlovability wound and a bunch of tangled wounds in previous incarnations with Markus. It was absolutely liberating. I also had two PowerShakes today, so I am ready to *go*."

"Well, it's showing. You look like a new version of yourself, Ronni. Damnit, I should have done an SG round before we headed to P-town. But even without it, maybe I can still meet my Ryan+ at this concert."

Veronica frowned as she glanced over at her sister. Although Ryan was attractive, Veronica couldn't help but feel that he was more of an accessory than the kind of Soul connection that she wished for her sister.

"Geez, don't give me that look, Ronni. I meant someone who has a pretty face and a hot body *like* Ryan, but *plus*—a deeper—shall we say, Soul connection, too. Yes, it's true, I'm starting to think that a sacred connection in love and romance *may be* a better benchmark to manifest than what I had been encouraging you towards. I can admit when I'm wrong." Margot reached over and squeezed her sister's hand.

Veronica squeezed her hand back, enlivened by the expansion she was seeing within Margot since she had said "yes" to her own authentic expansion. It was a Universal law she was beginning to realize—when you say yes to being your true self and took actions for it to be made manifest, those close to you were inspired to do the same.

As Margot accelerated on the Oregon Coast Highway and turned onto Highway 18 to head to Portland, a swooshing of Light engulfed Veronica's heart. She finally felt ready for whatever the outcome with Markus would be.

~

When Margot and Veronica arrived at the Aladdin Theater, they were surprised—Margot happily, Veronica nervously—to discover that the tickets Markus had left for them were in the very first row, in the middle of the aisle.

"I've never sat this close to the stage during a show. This is going to be so much fun Ronni," Margot said.

Veronica gasped. She would basically be sitting on Markus's lap for the concert. She was starting to think she should have given her ticket to Eloise who had wished her luck as she headed home to her kiddos after dinner with Veronica and Margot at Harlow. Veronica was also starting to second-guess her outfit. She glanced down at her black one-shoulder crop top, skinny jeans, and black peek-a-boo heels. Maybe she had dressed too suggestively. Further back, she would have blended in, but here in the front row, she could easily be mistaken for a groupie hoping for a one-night stand. Veronica fingered her beaded earrings, wishing they weren't so large and eye-catching. At least she had brought a wrap to drape over her and now she could potentially use it to cover up any embarrassment or shyness she might feel, she thought. With this seating arrangement, she and Markus would be practically staring right at one another. After what had occurred during his last concert, she was uncertain about the potential outcomes of being so close to him as he shared his musical gifts with the crowd.

Margot, seeming to read her thoughts, said, "Hey Ronni, don't worry, with the lights and everything, it's not like he'll be able to see only you. I've heard musicians and other performance artists say that with the lights on, they can only see a mass of faces, but nothing clearly. It's when they turn the house lights down that they can see more clearly. So, only get nervous about him watching you if *that* happens."

Veronica grimaced at her sister, who was simply trying to nurse her through any lingering insecurities.

Margot playfully elbowed Veronica and then said, "Come on, let's go check out their merch table before the show starts."

Once there, Veronica spotted a V-neck form-fitting indigo blue shirt by The Sunshine State that pulled at her.

"Why don't you just get it?" Margot asked.

"Again, not really going for that stalker vibe. If he tells me tonight after the concert that he wants to extend our connection beyond friendship, then I might get the shirt. Until then, I'm not making any moves."

"I swear, I've never seen you this wise when it comes to romance, Ronni," Margot said.

She was right. Veronica rarely had this kind of self-control and maturity in her romantic connections. She was either a bubbling schoolgirl giddy over a new connection, or she wasn't into it at all. With Markus, if he was ready to say "yes" to their relationship, may it be so, if not, well–Veronica hadn't gotten to that part yet in her mind but she was sure she'd think of something with the help and support of her spiritual team and Angelic family.

The lights blinked, and Margot and Veronica hurriedly made their way to their front-row seats. Veronica heard her phone ping and immediately pulled it out. It was a group text from her Angelics family. They sent a photo of all of them cheering in exuberant joy along with, "We're rooting for you and Markus! May the Light prevail and may Holy Beloved Sacred Union be yours! XOXO♥"

Veronica beamed. She felt so held and blessed by her spiritual physical family and her physical family, of which Margot was the sole member, not to mention her long-time dear friend Eloise. And that was perfect for her.

The Sunshine State came onto the stage and Markus looked right in her direction upon walking up to his microphone and guitar. This alone gave Veronica massive butterflies and made her heart soar–all at the same time. He wore his black button-up collared shirt with blue jeans and black Converse sneakers well. So well that she would've loved to run right up there and kiss his lovable face. That was the power of Markus Mullins, in full effect for her.

"I swear, he looked to make sure you were sitting here,"

Margot whispered. A shiver rippled through Veronica's body. She wanted so much to believe it was true, and not just wishful thinking.

As The Sunshine State played their most popular songs, Margot and Veronica joined the crowd in dancing and singing along. Veronica did her best not to stare endlessly at Markus, even though she thought she might have caught his eye a couple of times throughout the set.

"Hey, thank you so much everyone for being here with us tonight. We love playing the Aladdin and we're so thrilled you all came out to share your Friday night with us. We're gonna do something a little different at this show," Markus said, as his other two band members left the stage and the house lights went off.

"Oh my God! He turned the house lights off." Margot leaned over again, whispering loudly to Veronica as if she needed the narration of what was happening right in front of her.

A wave of nausea coupled with fluttering filled Veronica's stomach. She saw Markus glance down at her and smile, his gorgeous swoon-worthy smile.

"So tonight I want to share a bit more intimately with all of you something important that's been happening in my life. You all game for that?"

Screams of "Yes!!" and "We love you, Markus" echoed throughout the crowd.

Veronica, however, could do nothing more than keep her eyes locked on him. The fluttery butterfly sensations seemed to surround her now.

"Not too long ago, something wonderful happened to me. Someone special came into my life." He paused, scratching his head, seeming perplexed about what to say next. "You know what? This doesn't feel right like this. Hey Fred—" Markus called off the microphone to one of his stagehands. "Can you bring a chair out here for me?"

DR. HEATHER KRISTIAN STRANG

A few seconds later, a lanky young man with a ponytail delivered a tall high-back chair and set it next to him. Markus shifted his gaze to Veronica. "V, will you come up here please?"

As he said this, Fred put out a box set of stairs by the stage. Veronica shook her head frantically no. Not only did she have stage fright, but there was also no way she was going to be on stage next to Markus with thousands of people, cameras, videos, and lord knew what else happening. Daydreaming about being on stage with him and *actually being* on stage with him were two totally different things.

"Ronni, go up there!" Margot pushed her.

Veronica sat paralyzed, her peek-a-boo heels glued to the floor.

Markus continued, "Listen V, I can't. I can't talk about you and talk about what's been happening without talking *to* you. I need you up here with me. I know it's scary, but..." Markus scanned the crowd. "You all will be nice, right?"

The crowd responded with cheers and "Bring her up!"

Veronica looked around for her water bottle, her throat suddenly parched. This was like an out-of-body experience. How was she going to get up from her seat and walk onto that stage to talk to him in front of everyone?

Margot could see what was happening to her sister, and the level of fear she was experiencing, so she did what a good sister does. She took Veronica's purse and wrap, setting it on her own lap, and then nudged Veronica in a way that was imperceivable to anyone but Markus. Markus mouthed, "Thank you."

Markus tried again. "I know this is sort of awkward, V, but it's the only way. I have to tell you everything and I have to tell you now. I need you beside me for that to happen."

"Get on stage, V!!" a woman in the crowd yelled.

Margot tried a different tactic. "You got this, Ronni. I've got you, Markus has got you, this crowd has got you, and your spiritual family has got you."

Being reminded of all the support she had broke through

Veronica's haze and allowed her to slowly stand up and walk to the stage. The crowd erupted into applause. Markus met her at the stairs and extended his hand.

She could do this. She exhaled a cleansing breath, mentally tapped Cortices, and moved towards him. As she reached the top of the steps, Veronica clasped his hand and he wrapped his arms around her, whispering in her ear, "Thank you. I promise I'll make this worth your time."

She half-smiled, the butterfly sensations now replaced with wobbly, shaking legs and the fierce knowing that her focus at this moment could only be upon him, otherwise she might fall over. "Just keep your eyes on me. It's me and you," he said.

The crowd cheered as Markus led Veronica to the high-backed chair and lifted her onto it. He stood facing her, his hands on her waist, his eyes never leaving hers. "You look so utterly gorgeous tonight."

Veronica placed both of her hands on his face. She nodded. He nodded back in reply. Their telepathic communication was coming back online. It was time. Markus grabbed the microphone and turned to the crowd, holding Veronica's hand.

"I want you to meet the most special and sweet and kind and Angelic woman–Veronica."

The crowd went wild again, this time with screams of, "Hi Veronica!"

Veronica giggled, grateful that Markus was holding her hand and offering a steadying and grounding force. Even so, she was trembling, her mind incapable of anticipating what was coming next.

"Veronica came into my life not too long ago, and with it, she brought incredible magic. You know those things you call coincidences? They're not random, folks. They're synchronicities, and I believe that they're leading me and you to our highest Destiny, especially when you have the courage to follow them. Cuz that's the thing, these synchronicities will take you on all kinds of wild rides outside of your comfort zone, and that means you must follow them. I've had a hard time following it throughout my life. But I've come to realize..." He stared directly into Veronica's eyes. "I've come to realize that following the synchronicity leads to the best that life has to offer."

"Veronica, you are one of my synchronicities, and I know I told you I couldn't do this with you—"

The crowd audibly gasped, shocked to hear that Markus had shut her out.

He turned to the crowd, "I know, you're right. I was an idiot, plain and simple. But, cut me some slack guys, I am only human."

He looked over at Veronica and winked; they both knew he was far more than only human.

Veronica inhaled sharply and her gaze swept over the crowd. She glimpsed Margot holding her phone up, recording everything. Thank God. Her mind was so scrambled, she would never remember what he was saying. She was both in the moment and out of her body, watching what was happening. She released another deep, jagged breath, wanting to savor every morsel while also praying desperately that her legs and hands and every part of her would stop shaking.

Markus pivoted, fully facing Veronica now.

"I know who you are. I know why you've come into my life and why I've come into yours. I remember." Tears filled his eyes. "I'm sorry it took me as long as it did, but I'm here. I remember you, I remember us, and I'm ready for our life together."

Tears began running down Veronica's face. All along, the dreams, her intuition, the synchronicities, her Angelic family- all of it was, right. She hadn't been crazy, she hadn't been delusional, she hadn't been wanting something that wasn't hers to have. It was all right here for her and it was real. Waves of chills covered her from head to toe, and all she could do was stare into his eyes transmitting "I know, I know, I know. Thank you, thank you, thank you."

"I want to share this song with you that spontaneously came through me when I had the ecstatic experience of remembering you. Would that be okay with you?"

Veronica swallowed hard, speechless, as the tears rolled down her face. The synchronicities continued. At the first concert that she attended, uncontrollable tears had fallen down her face, but she had been confused. This time, the uncontrollable tears fell and she knew exactly what they meant. She loved Markus Mullins and he loved her too. And they were going to be together, of that she was certain.

Markus glanced at the crowd. "Would that be alright with you?"

Thousands of "YESSSS!!!" echoed throughout the concert hall.

Markus then picked up his guitar and played the most love-filled, harmonic song ever to have been played.

"This is for you, V," he said as he began to sing.

All of my life I knew you existed
  I could feel you in the early mornings and late nights
  All of my life I waited to meet you
  I couldn't wait to have you in my life

Your Angelic presence was foretold to me
  So many years ago, when I was but a boy
  Now here you are standing in front of me
  And I know with all certainty that you're mine

You're the one for me to hold endlessly
  You're the one for me to love deeply
  You're the one for me for all of eternity

. . .

All of my life I knew you existed
  And here you now are
  I can't believe it but I wouldn't want it any other way

Veronica – will you be mine?
  Forever now and forever thine?
  I am certain of this and only this
  A love like ours is forever made in Bliss.

Veronica was in full sobs as she watched the golden Light of Source fill Markus's eyes and the golden orb she had seen all that time ago above him as he played, now flowing into his entire being. The Light of Source encircling them both, and as he sang, she sensed an expansive portal of love opening between them. As he sang, she was both there in front of him and in the Angelic realm, united with him fully.

It caught her by surprise, but she noticed tears trickling down Markus's cheek as he sang to her. She saw him remembering even more who they were to each other as their eyes locked intently into one another. As Markus finished the song, he headed over to Veronica, placed both hands on her face, and kissed her fiercely. The entire crowd cheered, and Veronica could not believe that this was her life.

~

She couldn't stop smiling as Markus fumbled with the keys to open his front door.

"I don't know what it is about you tonight, V, but you're making me very nervous," he teased as he opened the door to his navy-colored Victorian home nestled in a tiny coastal neighborhood. Two weather-worn rocking chairs with engraved wood-cut flowers sat on the porch, a small table between them.

"Me? What about that trick you pulled tonight, forcing me to get up on stage in front of thousands of people? Talk about nervousness. I didn't think I was going to be able to walk up there. It was so hard for me."

As they stepped into his home, the energy between them filled the space with joy and Light. On the two-hour drive from Portland, they held hands regularly looking over at each other with a mix of both disbelief and bursting excitement. They hadn't said a whole lot. It was as if they were processing and integrating their energies with one another as they made their way to his home.

Veronica noticed that Markus's phone was buzzing repeatedly on the drive to his house. He had been sheepish at first about having to continually dismiss the calls when they came through. Finally, he explained to Veronica that his record label wasn't necessarily supportive of his performance that night.

"So, I had a call with the record label's executives about four weeks ago and while I thought they were going to scold me for some controversial song lyrics, they instead told me they wanted me to date an up-and-coming actress, Isabel Alvarez. They had researched and surmised that us being in the spotlight together would amplify both of our 'brands,'" Markus used air quotes with his hands to denote this, while also rolling his eyes as he glanced over at Veronica. She noticed a look of concern on his face as he shared this with her.

"Your record label can, uh, tell you who to date?"

"Well, technically no. But it happens a lot in the industry. It's very common that head execs coordinate relationships to further the artists' or actors' careers or to promote a new album or movie. I've gone along with this in the past here and there, and wouldn't you know it, right as we're meeting, they decide to try it again with me."

Veronica was quiet as she digested the information.

"Are these the same people who interfered in our first date at Salt?"

"Yes, sadly. I'm sure they can feel me distancing and when I spoke with them last, I was agitated by their interference in my life. It's been over a decade of this. I don't know how life-long celebrities handle this continual meddling and control in their personal and professional life." Markus sighed, running one of his hands through his hair.

Veronica had let some silence fill the space as she reflected on all that he was sharing with her. Her fingers trembled, this kind of interference was frightening, and she couldn't imagine how those in the spotlight handled it over and over again.

"What did you tell them you were going to do?" she eventually said, almost in a whisper, her fear getting the best of her.

"I told them I would think about it and let them know. Tonight's show was kind of, sort of me letting them know," he said with a grin.

Veronica burst into laughter. "Hell of a way to say no thanks to the arranged celeb romance, eh?"

"I feel like it was perfectly in line with my brand," he joked.

"I couldn't agree more," she replied, and then Markus had reached over, interlacing his fingers with hers.

Now that they were at his home, the record label drama avoided for the time being, all Veronica could feel was the heat of their connection increasing with every step they took. Markus set down his things as Veronica removed her black and red wrap. He watched her intently as she did. Veronica looked around at his artfully decorated home, filled with massive colorful paintings on every wall, along with a record player, musical instruments, and antique, yet stylish furnishings. His home looked a lot like something that should be featured in *Dwell* magazine.

"You're so stunning," he said softly.

Markus scooped her up into his arms and she instinctively

wrapped her legs around his waist. Looking into his eyes her cheeks rosy with love and joy and lust, she began kissing him, letting her tongue entwine with his. He began walking, surely steering them to a more appropriate location, although Veronica would have made love to him right there on the living room floor. All she cared about was being in his arms for as long as possible. Eventually, they made their way into his bedroom and he gently laid her on his bed.

Veronica licked her lips, hungry for more. She wasn't sure exactly what was happening, but it was as if tonight's events had turned the dial all the way up on their connection. She wanted him now more than she ever did, and she was beyond ready to be his.

Markus peeled off his shirt, revealing his toned chest and abdomen, and Veronica shuddered; he was spectacular. He reached over and began unbuttoning her jeans with confidence.

"Now, you know what this means," he said as he reached the end of the buttons.

Veronica stared up at him curiously.

"It means that I'm yours and you're mine. It means that when we merge our bodies as Angelics that our eternal timeline is activated and our lives will never be the same again."

Veronica leaned into him, kissing him slowly. "I wouldn't want it any other way," she whispered into his mouth.

After they made love, Veronica felt something she had never experienced before. The orgasmic bliss from when their bodies were merged continued, a steady flow of ecstasy cascading through her body as she lay in Markus's arms. When he first entered her, she felt a beam of Light move through her entire body and radiate out of her heart, flowing into his heart, and when their tongues touched at the same time, the Light created a circuit that flowed through both of their bodies.

Laying in his arms, Veronica spoke up. "By the way how did you know we were both Angelics and what our unified field would create when we merged? I only recently started learning about all of this when I remembered you at your concert a few months back. But you, how did you know?"

Markus looked over at her; a peace had washed over him that relaxed his face into what almost seemed Angelic as Veronica stared up at him.

"When I was very young, I had a dream–I mentioned this briefly in my song to you tonight–and in that dream, an Angel came to me. He told me that I was also from the Angelic realm and that at some point on my journey, I would unite with my Holy Beloved. Now there were times throughout my life that I dismissed this as being true and pretended that I didn't know who I really was. But when I had the time to reflect on our connection, I received incredible clarity. Clarity that not only was this dream I had as a child accurate, but that you were that Holy Beloved that I was shown existed for me."

He paused as he gently caressed her skin.

"Do you want to know how I knew it was you?" he asked.

"Um, yes. Please. My spiritual team made it pretty obvious to me that it was you, so yeah, I wanna hear what was revealed to you, too."

"Well, in that dream that I had as a child, the Angel showed me a girl with black, corkscrew curls and fair skin."

Veronica immediately sat up.

"No! He did not," she said.

"Yesssss," he said deliberately.

"Had you forgotten this when we met?"

He nodded, pulling her closer to him. "I hadn't thought about that dream in a long time. I had carried it with me until about college, always paying attention if ever I saw a woman with black curly hair and fair skin, but by the time college hit, I sort of gave up. I had a long-time college girlfriend who was blonde and blue-eyed, and I convinced myself that maybe that dream was just the idle ramblings of a young kid. I certainly didn't know anyone else who was having Angel's visit them."

Veronica loved being wrapped up in his arms, a maroon cashmere blanket laying over them both.

"I did notice as a child that I had some intuitive abilities and gifts, like I could almost see the thoughts visually of my parents and others around me. You know like how in comics there are word bubbles coming out of characters mouths? That's what I would see when people talked, only I'd see images and colors of what they really meant, even if they weren't being honest with their words. As an adult, if I thought about something enough and put intention behind it daily for twenty-two days—I came to the twenty-two days after many experimentations—then it would happen. I mean, that's how the success of my band happened. I did an opening prayer, and then I did a meditative prayer every day for twenty-two days to activate our success. And then it happened. So when things like that occurred, I would have moments of 'Yeah, maybe I am an Angel in form' because my bandmates and friends didn't have those kinds of gifts as far as I knew."

"This is extraordinary Markus. My Angelic family—whom I cannot wait to introduce you to—have told me that once you and I come together, our gifts and abilities will expand, and that we'll be able to create more powerfully together than we ever could as individuals. What do you think about that?"

They were both rolled onto their sides now, facing each other and talking. Veronica felt so comfortable with Markus that she didn't mind being openly naked in front of him, allowing her ample breasts and tummy to be on full display. She wasn't sucking in her stomach or thinking about how her body might look to him. She was fully herself and fully present with him.

Markus agreed. "That has been my sense, although I haven't received any direct communication from anyone about it. It would make sense as eternal beloveds. I believe you call us Divine Counterparts. Is that right?"

Veronica lovingly stroked a curl from his forehead, "Yes, that's right love."

He continued. "It would make sense that our coming together would allow us to create at a far larger level and that our gifts would expand as well. It gets me curious about what we are to create together and to learn more about our mission."

"Me too! Do you feel clear about your individual mission? I think that might give us a clue if we look at both of our individual missions. From what I've been shown, they combine to form a shared joint mission."

"Mmm...yes, good point, my love." He leaned over and gave her a simmering kiss. "You're so wise, V. Yeah, I've felt my whole life that my mission is to provide healing and joy through music. What do you feel yours is?"

Veronica sat with it for a minute, and she had to be honest. "You know, I never viewed my life like that until recently. When I was younger, I had this deep knowing that I had a Divine Love and that always felt like my destiny. But like you, I gave up after life did not present that love to me. I always felt an insatiable call to own a bookstore, and that desire propelled me into the job I have now working for Henry at Books on the Beach. And working there introduced me to my Angelic family..." Veronica trailed off as heat rose in her body and a whoosh of energy spiraled through her, starting at her spine, moving up to her chest, and then to her crown. She closed her eyes.

Markus reached out and touched her arm. "What are you feeling V, what's happening?"

Just then Veronica was whisked away to a scene in her minds-eye. She saw a large bookstore with organic superfood drinks and organic teas, along with Markus's records and metaphysical books and Markus playing music there. She saw bright, eclectic art on the walls and a community gathering space. She saw her favorite authors and musicians leading events; a music studio in the back where Markus recorded his music and helped other musicians with their work; a home living space above the bookstore café where she and Marcus lived; and a rooftop greenhouse. She saw a solar system, wood stove and rainwater catchment too. Veronica thought she heard little feet running through the space, as well.

She then glimpsed an image of a solo album of Markus's. She saw the cover clearly; it was simply his face in black and white up close with his name spelled out in a script font. An overwhelming love surged through her. They were doing what they loved most and were having a positive effect on humans. More humans were remembering who they really were by being in the presence of Markus's music and their shop. Pink and golden energy emanated from their bookstore-juice bar-music venue out into the blue sky and ocean waters.

When the imagery was complete, Veronica's eyes popped open, and she felt a wave of dizziness. "Oh my God, Markus. I think I was just shown our mission, or what we are to create together. It brings in our individual passions and desires and takes them to a whole new level. Holy. Wow."

As she took several intentional breaths, Markus kept his hand on Veronica's arm, as if he knew his touch grounded her. She carefully shared the details of her vision, uncertain how he would feel about it as Markus had been a touring musician for his entire career. To her, it seemed like the most fulfilling, satisfying life she could ever hope for. She held her breath, wondering if he felt the same.

He watched her as she shared in detail about the vision.

"Whoa, I'm covered in chills." Markus lifted his arm to show her the hairs raising on end and the goosebumps that surfaced from his skin.

"Right? It felt like, I can't even find the words, but wow, so incredible. How would you feel if this was our shared mission? What about touring with your music?" Veronica asked hesitantly.

Markus paused for a moment, rolling onto his back, gazing up at the ceiling.

"You know, the music industry is changing so much: the way we make music, how we distribute our music, all of it. I can see still playing shows as we're called to." He reached out and grabbed her hand. "You going with me would be a priority." Veronica loved the sound of that.

"And what you describe is exactly the kind of expansion I can see for myself. Producing my own music, helping other artists, finding creative ways to get our music out into the world, and moving beyond the hierarchical control system that runs the media and music of this world. I've also wanted to bring in healing harmonies to my music like 432hz and 528hz. These musical frequencies are directly tied to the pulse of the Earth, which heals the human body and mind. Maybe it *is* time to break away from my band and have more of my creations be solo, and then do occasional albums or events with them every few years or so."

Veronica could not believe, but she also *could* believe, how in sync they were and how their mission was being shown to them. And this was all happening after night one of them both saying YES to merging their bodies and therefore sharing the rest of their incarnation together.

She sighed as Markus pulled her snugly into his arms. "Is that a yes, my love?"

She giggled. "Yes" as his lips met hers and they pressed their naked bodies into one another, igniting a circuit of golden Light between them and all around them.

CHAPTER 13

Veronica knocked gently on the door. "We're here!" she said as she opened it slightly.

Henry rushed to let them in. "Oh, come in, come in," he said excitedly as Veronica and Markus entered his home.

"You must be Markus," Henry said. "We've been eagerly waiting to meet you, brother." He and Markus shook hands and hugged as though they were long-lost friends from another time.

Veronica and Markus shifted their focus to the great room where everyone was gathered, their faces lit up by the sight of Markus.

"He's here!" Cecilia let out a squeal, and she and Edward came over, followed by Meghan and Eric. Soft ambient music filtered into the space from Henry's sound system and white votive candles gave the space a heavenly glow.

Traditional handshakes and formalities were replaced with hugs as they each felt a sense of knowing one another before. Markus put his arm around Veronica's waist, whispering, "It's just like you said it would be. I definitely feel as though I know them already."

Markus turned to face them as everyone prepared to sit down for their weekly meditation.

"I can't help but feel as though I'm remembering each of you, just as I also remembered V. She's told me so much about how you supported her through her remembering me and my lag in remembering as quickly." He chuckled, then turned serious. "Thank you. Thank you for taking care of my Holy Beloved Divine Counterpart. Thank you for believing in me. Thank you for believing in us."

Veronica noticed tears in the eyes of her Angelic family. Meghan and Eric were in their usual place on the floor with their blanket cozied up, and Edward was in his same spot sitting on a cushion leaned up against the couch Cecilia was on. Veronica and Markus took their seats opposite Cecilia and Edward on the leather couch, and Henry was of course in his white meditation chair. Tonight's meditation was certainly going to take everyone to a new level.

Suddenly, Henry's face sobered. "But Markus, there have been some new attempts to interfere with your union with Veronica, yes?"

He asked this as a question but said it in a way that was also a statement. Markus blinked seeming surprised by this, while Veronica was only mildly shocked that Henry had instantaneously tuned into the negative energy present in Markus's field. She leaned over to Markus. "Remember, us Angelics are very psychic, and Henry is one of the best."

Markus smiled nervously at the rest of his Angelic family. "So is this like a hazard in the Angelic family–everyone intuits everyone else's life?"

Cecilia, Meghan, Eric, and Edward shrugged.

"Having superpowers can be annoying at times but usually we're only shown information when we can be of help to each other," Edward answered.

Markus took a sharp breath. "I was hoping to take care of this on my own, but as Henry has intuited, yes, there has been some increasing pressure from my record label to terminate my relationship with Veronica since we unified as one. I do feel I'm being asked to choose the label and follow what they demand, or move powerfully onto my own path with V," Markus said.

"I'm so sorry honey. I hate that this is happening," Veronica said quietly, placing her forehead against his temple. Markus had recently heard from Katie that despite his union with Veronica, the label was still planning to leak to the press that he was in a relationship with Isabel.

"You know, this is all quite normal, although a bit more intense because of your fame," Cecilia spoke up. "When Edward and I were coming together, we had massive interference from our children from our previous marriages, and even our exes were pulling out all the stops to pressure us to abandon our path together."

Meghan agreed. "Same with Eric and me. I had to quit my job of five years in accounting because for some 'unexplained' reason they suddenly wanted me working twenty-four-seven once Eric and I came together. And let's not even talk about my parents. You all know even recently I was dealing with their shenanigans in trying to break Eric and me apart."

Markus seemed shocked. Henry spoke next. "Yes, the artificial matrix knows that with every Angelic couple that comes together, their power is ten times greater than when they're solo. So the agenda works overtime through friends, family, employers, and to your point Markus, record labels, to interfere in the union. What's most important is that you both hold strong, placing your union at the top position in your focus. It's important to double your meditation and prayer time together and take actions that will allow you to practice ceremony and ritual regularly together. It can also be helpful to have some energy healing done to clear out the psychic interference."

"I also highly recommend taking sea salt baths together too," Eric chimed in. Everyone giggled in agreement.

"Definitely, a must," Meghan confirmed.

"Why sea salt?" Markus asked.

"Sea salt clears your auric or energy field so that the psychic daggers, interferences, and debris can be cleared out. When you take the bath together it clears the field for your union, obviously," Henry said with a chuckle.

"Oookay, so we absolutely have some practices to get to work on," Veronica said, as she placed her hand on Markus's thigh.

"So, do these attempts ever work to keep Angelics apart?" Markus asked.

"Sadly, they do at times," said Henry. "If Angelics don't have family support like we all are blessed to have with each other, it's quite difficult to face these psychic attacks and attempts to break apart the union. In the face of so much pressure and without practices and assistance, some of our brothers and sisters have failed to unite because of this. It's a terrible loss for us all as an Angelic family when this happens, but also for the collective consciousness. That's one less couple, with ten times the superpowers to assist the transformation of Earth from a dualistic plane of good versus evil to a place of Immense Love."

"Wow," was all Veronica could say.

She felt even more grateful to have been united with her Angelic family before coming together with Markus. There was no way she would have been able to withstand the pressure by herself. She wondered how Markus would hold up in all of this.

As if reading her mind, Markus traced her cheek with his finger. "I had a successful, decades-long music career in the mainstream. It served my human ego well. But now, I need and want more. And I want it with you, V. I want our vision, I want our mission, I want to spend the next however many more decades we get on Earth–together."

Meghan and Cecilia began clapping, and Eric, Edward, and Henry beamed over at them. Henry leaned over to pat Markus on the back and Edward came over and embraced him. Eric leaned in to give Markus a fist bump of solidarity.

Veronica wiped tears from her eyes.

"Oh thank Goddess," she said as she wrapped her arms around Markus.

After the meditation, everyone's face was glowing and relaxed.

"Our Angelic family is growing, and I can feel one more Soul wanting to join us very soon," Meghan said with joy.

"One more? Very soon?" Veronica asked.

All eyes turned to Henry, who pretended not to notice and looked in the other direction. It was Eric who spoke up next.

"Well, there's still at least one more of us who's to unite with their Holy Beloved Divine Counterpart here on Earth. And who knows, more family members could reveal themselves as well, as our Angelic family could easily expand to eleven or twenty-two Souls. In any event, I'm sure that things will start moving along quite quickly now that Veronica and Markus are united."

Henry was examining his timer intently, seemingly oblivious to what was going on and acting as though he was calculating tremendous data based upon their meditation.

"Oh! So we gotta now help Henry like you all helped V," Markus said.

All heads in the room bobbed up and down quickly, while Henry again acted as though he had no idea what was happening.

He glanced up, doe-eyed and innocent. "So, shall we have some dessert? I made superfood energy balls with Veronica's Purium Chai Spice Protein for everyone tonight."

Markus laughed softly. "Henry, I see you man, and I'm here for you. We all are."

Henry grimaced, clearly uncomfortable being the center of

attention as someone who needed support. He was far more comfortable serving as a mentor and guide for his spiritual family. He let out an exaggerated breath and said, "Well, my situation is a whole lot more complicated, and there's no need to quickly move our focus off of the glory that is Markus and Veronica coming together..."

"Oh my God," Meghan said, her face ashen.

"What...what is it?" Veronica said as Meghan nodded for her to look closely at Henry.

"Use your spiritual sight, Veronica," Cecilia whispered.

Markus squeezed Veronica's hand, clearly aware of whatever the others were noticing.

Veronica narrowed her eyes so she could see beyond the physical. She gasped at the outline of a beautiful woman with long flowing hair standing behind Henry, her hands placed upon his shoulders.

Tears brimmed in Henry's eyes, while Meghan, Eric, Cecilia, and Edward said in unison, "And so it begins."

The End

WILDEST DREAMS JOURNEY
CONTINUES...

Your *Wildest Dreams* Journey continues with the resources Markus & Veronica used to activate their Angelic selves:

- **Veronica's go-to balancing tool**. Free Cortices video to balance the left and right hemispheres of your brain, allowing greater access to your Higher Self: **bit.ly/Cortices222**
- **Purium organic Superfoods, including V's body-changing PowerShake**. Get $50-off your first order with coupon code: MetaphysicalMenu
- Start with the Core 4 or Markus's fave, the 90-day Health Reset: **bit.ly/PuriumSuperfoods**
- **Intuitive food blog** that Markus tells Veronica about: **metaphysicalmenu.com/recipes-recommends/**
- **Free Golden Age meditation** to join our weekly Sunday remote group meditation – imagine you're in Henry's living room with us! **bit.ly/ GoldenAgeMeditation**
- **Superpowers Guide**, including the potent Inner Child self-healing process that Veronica used to

prepare for Markus: **sacred-spirituality.org/ activate-your-highly-sensitive-superpowers- guide/**

- *A Life Of Magic: A Spirit-Led Oracle, Ecstatic Union with The Divine, Live Like You're On Vacation Oracles* channeled by Dr. Strang and **recommended to V by Margot.** Get the series here: **amzn.to/3Zaw6M3**

ACKNOWLEDGMENTS

Thank you, dear reader, for saying "yes" to this Angelics journey with me! I'm so grateful to my Higher Self who had me knowing at age 12 that I was here on Earth to be a writer. I'm so grateful to all of the people and experiences in my life that inspired this story and The Way that the entire storyline and characters developed themselves as I typed.

I'm so grateful to my writing coaches Barbara and Ramy for their guidance and support. Thank you to my beta reader Lara for confirming all that my spiritual team had shown me about this book. Thank you to my wonderful editor Stacy for your help in bringing this book into full form. Thank you to my love E for his endless encouragement and belief in my ability to write this story, and the stories to come.

I'm so over-the-moon grateful to Source HerSelf and my spiritual team for all of the synchronicity, magic and love that I've been blessed to experience since my spiritual awakening in 2008. Thank you to Veronica, Markus, Henry, Meghan, Eric, Cecilia, Edward, and Margot. I didn't know you would be here with me and be as magnificent as you are. Thank you for coming into my life and into the lives of all of our readers.

Blessed be and may all Angelics unite with their Holy Beloved Divine Counterparts and their Angelic families in form, here upon Earth. And so it is. It is so. XO

About the Author

Dr. Heather Kristian Strang is a mystic, metaphysical psychologist and an Amazon bestselling author. She's written 12 books in the genres of visionary fiction, paranormal romance, and channeled message Oracles—basically, everything she loves, she writes about!

Kristian has been featured in publications such as *Bustle, The Huffington Post, Elephant Journal, Thrive Global, Elite Daily,* and on the cover of the *Sedona Journal of Emergence.* She's also been a featured speaker on a number of podcasts and summits, including her own podcast, *Awakening: The Podcast.*

When she's not doing all of that, you'll find her dance-walking on the Oregon Coast or baking it up in the kitchen for her high-vibe nutrition blog, *Metaphysical Menu*. You can also receive free meditations and transmissions, and learn about Dr. Kristian's trainings & certifications at:

http://www.Sacred-Spirituality.org

THANK YOU FOR READING MY BOOK!

I value your feedback and I would love to hear what you have to say about *The Angelics: Wildest Dreams*!

Please take two minutes now to leave a helpful review on Amazon or my website letting me know how *The Angelics Wildest Dreams* blessed and impacted you. What was your favorite part? What would you like to see happen next in the series?

Thank you so much! XoKristian

Made in the USA
Columbia, SC
20 May 2024

35898578R00131